G R JORDAN
Someone Else's Ritual
A Highlands and Islands Detective Thriller #43

First published by Carpetless Publishing 2025

Copyright © 2025 by G R Jordan

All rights reserved. No part of this publication may be reproduced, stored or transmitted in any form or by any means, electronic, mechanical, photocopying, recording, scanning, or otherwise without written permission from the publisher. It is illegal to copy this book, post it to a website, or distribute it by any other means without permission.

This novel is entirely a work of fiction. The names, characters and incidents portrayed in it are the work of the author's imagination. Any resemblance to actual persons, living or dead, events or localities is entirely coincidental.

G R Jordan asserts the moral right to be identified as the author of this work.

G R Jordan has no responsibility for the persistence or accuracy of URLs for external or third-party Internet Websites referred to in this publication and does not guarantee that any content on such Websites is, or will remain, accurate or appropriate.

Designations used by companies to distinguish their products are often claimed as trademarks. All brand names and product names used in this book and on its cover are trade names, service marks, trademarks and registered trademarks of their respective owners. The publishers and the book are not associated with any product or vendor mentioned in this book. None of the companies referenced within the book have endorsed the book.

For avoidance of doubt, no part of this publication may be used in any manner for purposes of training artificial intelligence technologies to generate text, including without limitation, technologies that are capable of generating works in the same style or genre as the Work.

First edition

ISBN (print): 978-1-917497-19-0
ISBN (digital): 978-1-917497-18-3

This book was professionally typeset on Reedsy.
Find out more at reedsy.com

Archaeology is not what you find, it's what you find out.

> DAVID HURST THOMAS,
> ARCHAEOLOGIST

Contents

Foreword	iii
Acknowledgments	iv
Books by G R Jordan	v
Chapter 01	1
Chapter 02	10
Chapter 03	18
Chapter 04	27
Chapter 05	36
Chapter 06	44
Chapter 07	53
Chapter 08	63
Chapter 09	72
Chapter 10	81
Chapter 11	91
Chapter 12	101
Chapter 13	110
Chapter 14	119
Chapter 15	127
Chapter 16	135
Chapter 17	143
Chapter 18	152
Chapter 19	162
Chapter 20	171
Chapter 21	179

Chapter 22	186
Chapter 23	194
Chapter 24	201
Chapter 25	211
Read on to discover the Patrick Smythe series!	219
About the Author	222
Also by G R Jordan	224

Foreword

The events of this book, while based around real and also fictitious locations around the UK and Europe, are entirely fictional and all characters do not represent any living or deceased person. All companies are fictitious representations and locations have been modified for the purposes of the story. This novel is best read while inside a tunnel but with the bomb diffused!

Acknowledgments

To Ken, Jean, Colin, Evelyn, John and Rosemary for your work in bringing this novel to completion, your time and effort is deeply appreciated.

Books by G R Jordan

The Highlands and Islands Detective series (Crime)

1. Water's Edge
2. The Bothy
3. The Horror Weekend
4. The Small Ferry
5. Dead at Third Man
6. The Pirate Club
7. A Personal Agenda
8. A Just Punishment
9. The Numerous Deaths of Santa Claus
10. Our Gated Community
11. The Satchel
12. Culhwch Alpha
13. Fair Market Value
14. The Coach Bomber
15. The Culling at Singing Sands
16. Where Justice Fails
17. The Cortado Club
18. Cleared to Die
19. Man Overboard!
20. Antisocial Behaviour
21. Rogues' Gallery
22. The Death of Macleod - Inferno Book 1

23. A Common Man - Inferno Book 2
24. A Sweeping Darkness - Inferno Book 3
25. Dormie 5
26. The First Minister - Past Mistakes Book 1
27. The Guilty Parties - Past Mistakes Book 2
28. Vengeance is Mine - Past Mistakes Book 3
29. Winter Slay Bells
30. Macleod's Cruise
31. Scrambled Eggs
32. The Esoteric Tear
33. A Rock 'n' Roll Murder
34. The Slaughterhouse
35. Boomtown
36. The Absent Sculptor
37. A Trip to Rome
38. A Time to Rest
39. Cinderella's Carriage
40. Wild Swimming
41. The Wrong Man
42. Drop Like Flies
43. Someone Else's Ritual
44. None Too Precious
45. Save the King (releasing 2025)
46. The Silent War (releasing 2025)

Kirsten Stewart Thrillers (Thriller)

1. A Shot at Democracy
2. The Hunted Child
3. The Express Wishes of Mr MacIver
4. The Nationalist Express
5. The Hunt for 'Red Anna'
6. The Execution of Celebrity
7. The Man Everyone Wanted
8. Busman's Holiday
9. A Personal Favour
10. Infiltrator
11. Implosion
12. Traitor

Jac Moonshine Thrillers

1. Jac's Revenge
2. Jac for the People
3. Jac the Pariah

Siobhan Duffy Mysteries

1. A Giant Killing
2. Death of the Witch
3. The Bloodied Hands
4. A Hermit's Death

The Contessa Munroe Mysteries (Cozy Mystery)

1. Corpse Reviver
2. Frostbite
3. Cobra's Fang

The Patrick Smythe Series (Crime)

1. The Disappearance of Russell Hadleigh
2. The Graves of Calgary Bay
3. The Fairy Pools Gathering

Austerley & Kirkgordon Series (Fantasy)

1. Crescendo!
2. The Darkness at Dillingham
3. Dagon's Revenge
4. Ship of Doom

Supernatural and Elder Threat Assessment Agency (SETAA) Series (Fantasy)

1. Scarlett O'Meara: Beastmaster

Island Adventures Series (Cosy Fantasy Adventure)

1. Surface Tensions

Dark Wen Series (Horror Fantasy)

1. The Blasphemous Welcome
2. The Demon's Chalice

Chapter 01

'Are you excited?'

Clarissa Urquhart gave a glance at DCI Seoras Macleod. She wasn't sure if he was joking or not. He did that every now and again. He said things in a voice that made you wonder.

'I'm always excited around you,' said Clarissa, and gave a smile back.

'But are they ready? Are you sure they can cover this?'

'Well, they're going to have to, aren't they? You're the one who wants me on the other job. You're the one that wants me to dig out the background on the knife. So yes, they'll be ready for it. Besides, she knows her art.'

'And him?'

'Well, he's not green, and he might not know art inside out, but he's got her. He'll be good, though. He'll know how to follow things through.'

Clarissa opened the office door in one of Glasgow's police stations. A sign on it read, *Arts Division*. She had wondered about the frosty reception they might have got, given the recent past, and how Sabine had been received—even Perry. With that in mind, she had picked Lemon for the post.

A man in a tailored—but not ostentatious—suit stood up. Clarissa noticed his shoes were polished, so much so she could probably see her face in them. His hair was cut short, and there was hardly an ounce of fat on him. He was muscly too, arms pressing against the suit. Not too much, though. Just enough so you knew they were there.

'Sam,' said Clarissa. 'This is DCI Seoras Macleod.'

'Absolute pleasure to meet you, sir,' said Sam, reaching out with a hand.

'It's just Seoras these days.'

'Ex-military,' Clarissa said.

'Yes, sir. Sorry. Hard to drop it when you've been in there.'

'Military police?'

'Yes, but now out due to some job cuts.' He almost winced when he said it.

'Well, their loss, our gain. You happy enough? Clarissa's explained the situation, has she?'

'Yes, she has, and to my colleague . . .' Sam looked around. 'I'm afraid she nipped out for a moment.'

'It's not a problem,' said Clarissa. 'Take it easy, Sam.'

'Did you want any donuts?' a voice said behind Macleod. He turned, and a young woman almost floated into the room behind him. He would have described her as large-built, not unkindly. Just a woman who was 'big-boned,' as they said back in the day.

She was carrying a tray of donuts and coffees in her hand and gave a large, almost apologetic smile as she saw Clarissa with Macleod. She wore a large baggy jumper with jeans underneath and boots that came halfway up her shin.

'You must be the Detective Chief Inspector. Did you want a donut as well?'

CHAPTER 01

'This is DC Erin Light,' said Clarissa. 'Erin, this is Detective Chief Inspector Seoras Macleod.'

'Delighted to meet you,' said Erin. 'Donut?'

'Don't mind if I do,' said Macleod, smiling.

'Bring those in, Erin,' said Sam. 'Sir, would you like—sorry, Seoras—would you like to sit down?'

Macleod was offered a seat and doughnuts passed around. A rather dapper-looking man wearing a cravat entered.

'Sam, Erin, this is Pats.'

'I'm DC Eric Patterson. Eric's fine.'

'Nonsense,' said Clarissa. 'It's Pats. Pats, you call him. Okay. Pats, Sam Lemon, DS, and Erin Light, DC—your colleagues. If you've got any questions about the arts, Erin's the girl. Absolute genius on it. Could challenge me.'

Patterson raised his eyebrows.

'A little green on the detective front,' said Clarissa, 'but that's why Sam's here. Sam will keep you right, Erin. Not a lot on at the moment. Not expecting much. However, I have to go off for a small procedure. It's going to keep me out of action for about a month, possibly. Pats is also due some leave. He works terribly hard, don't you, Pats?' said Clarissa. 'You'll be okay with that, Sam?'

'You'll be running the investigations while Clarissa's away,' said Macleod. 'I'll be on the end of the phone, and if need be, I can appear. We have some others with experience of the arts world up in Inverness who could drop by, but I'd rather not step on your toes.'

'Thank you, sir,' said Sam.

'Just Seoras,' said Macleod.

'Well, team,' said Clarissa, 'this will be us in about a month. Till then it's you, Sam and Erin. The biggest thing you've got on at the moment is counterfeit selling, so get yourselves out around the auction marts, get in, and see if you spot anything coming up. Most of it's low level. There's nothing particularly exciting going on.'

Patterson looked away, out the window.

'Would you not agree?' asked Sam of Patterson.

'The boss is right,' responded Patterson. 'There's nothing on in Glasgow other than some counterfeiting.'

Sam watched Patterson closely before turning back to Clarissa, who was all smiles.

'Well, the very best,' said Sam. And then he stopped. 'Do I use Clarissa?'

'They do sometimes call you Macleod's—'

'Pats,' said Clarissa. 'That's enough. You can call me boss,' said Clarissa. 'I don't mind Clarissa either. Never Urquhart.'

'Not unless you're angry with her,' said Macleod. He stood up, Sam joined him, and they shook hands. 'All the best, Sergeant, Detective Constable. Do us proud. The DI's chosen well. Sorry, but I must get back up the road. Meetings and that. I'll leave Clarissa with you for five minutes.'

Clarissa joined Macleod in her car in the car park ten minutes later. They got into her green sports car and made their way back up the A9 towards Inverness.

'Looks a good team,' said Macleod.

'They are. They'll be fine. I'd like to be here for a while with them but as you've got me off chasing after this knife.'

'Pat's not coming with us then?' asked Macleod.

'No, part of the plan.'

'Well then, do you want to tell me about it?'

'Kirsten helped me make it out. I have to be honest. I'm not that keen on having her about.'

CHAPTER 01

Kirsten Stewart, former detective constable and British service agent, was helping Clarissa in trying to discover the origins of a ritualistic knife. It had been used to murder members of a supposed secret society. The society was believed to have influenced events, and acted in destroying criminal gangs. Sometimes they had dispatched others who crossed their path who weren't criminals. They'd also killed Gavin Isbister, a former colleague of Macleod's.

'What's your issue with Kirsten?'

'Ex-Service. Don't work like us, do they?'

'It wasn't because you replaced her. You know you didn't replace her. You just were the next person on the team.'

Clarissa glared at him.

'You couldn't have replaced Kirsten,' said Macleod. 'She was my protector. She would stand in front of me to fight other people. Had a mind like mine. She was—'

'You know how to build a girl up, don't you?'

'Well, I do speak well of her, at times,' said Macleod.

'No, I'm talking about me. She was all this. I was what? Nothing?'

'You were a wise old—' Macleod stopped.

'What?' said Clarissa.

'I was going to say mule, but—'

She punched him. 'You need not refer to me as a mule. In today's force, you could get done for that.'

'But you kicked like one,' said Macleod. 'Hard, unrelenting. You don't care. I've no qualms, no regrets about bringing you on to my team. You saved my life,' said Macleod. 'You went to places and off-piste to save my life. Hope wouldn't have done that. Hope couldn't have done that, but Kirsten's special. She knows a lot. She may be young, but she'll protect you.'

'Thought I was the rottweiler,' said Clarissa. 'I don't need protecting.'

'What way are you going about this, now that we're out in the car on our own?' asked Macleod.

'Well, I've got a contact on the occult, not one I use that often. We'll see him first. Find out if he has any ideas of where the markings on the knives and the knife comes from. You must realise, Seoras, that those who wield something like this—and I mean wield, not collect, wield it—they were using it in conjunction with a ceremony, an act. They'll have religious tendencies.'

'I do come from the Isle of Lewis. I know a lot about religion.'

'Do they have those sorts of tendencies up there?' asked Clarissa. 'Can't remember any ritual sacrifices.'

'Sacrifices are not always done with a knife. Or on show,' said Macleod, almost bitterly.

'Anyway, the plan is, I go in for a day for my hospital operation, or rather pretend operation, and come back a day or two later. I'll head off while I'm supposedly recovering at home.'

'How is it working, then?' asked Macleod. 'If you're meant to be going into hospital, there'll be records. People could look.'

'Private, and there'll be somebody there, getting an op done,' said Clarissa.

Macleod looked at her. 'Your old friend, Kirsten, went to Anna Hunt about it. The doctors won't know it's not me, paperwork will say one thing, the person who's going in needs this, and can't afford it. I think Kirsten played on Anna's caring side.'

'I wasn't aware Anna Hunt had a caring side,' said Macleod.

CHAPTER 01

Anna Hunt was head of the Service—a British spy network—the former boss of Kirsten, and someone Macleod trusted to a point.

'We'll keep in contact,' said Clarissa. 'Kirsten said she can contact you in ways that won't use any of the main police systems. But we may be dark for a bit. Pats is off on leave, so she's briefed him on how to disappear. We'll meet him somewhere down in England and get ourselves on the go. Another three or four days, and it'll all be happening.'

Macleod had parked at Clarissa's house in Inverness before they travelled to Glasgow. They now returned there. Frank strode out from the house as they arrived. He came up to shake Macleod's hand and took Clarissa inside. In the front living room, behind the closed curtains, sat Kirsten Stewart. She was diminutive in the sense that she wasn't tall, but she was as fit as a fiddle, in great shape and with long, flowing black hair running around her back. Clarissa looked at her and grimaced.

One of the hard things about being older was when these younger pups came in. It was bad enough that they were fitter. And yes, they looked better than you. Of course they did, but the girl had no style. A jumper and jeans. Not like Clarissa. Although Kirsten had said Clarissa would have to ditch her style for this investigation.

'Everything all right, Frank?' she asked.

'Kirsten's been briefing me. Once you go in and come back out and then disappear, I'll be entertaining your colleagues, pretending to come and make sure you're okay. We're all set. I'm good with it.'

'There's a redhead woman that you might see about,' said Kirsten. 'I had to tell Anna Hunt something. She doesn't know the full details of what we're doing, though she'll guess. But she had the decency to offer to put someone here, just in case anyone comes looking for you,' Kirsten said to Clarissa. 'I want to make sure that if anyone comes to see if you're here, they'll be taken care of. Frank won't get moved unless we have to.'

Clarissa stepped forward and put her arms around Frank's shoulders. 'Are you okay with this? If you're not, I walk.'

He turned and looked her up and down. 'You obviously think this is important. It's not just the art this time, is it?'

She shook her head. 'I can't go into all the details,' she said.

'Clearly,' said Frank. 'It must be serious. Kirsten's here. Kirsten can really handle herself by the looks of it.'

'I'm sure Clarissa can handle herself, too,' said Kirsten.

'I'll have Pats with me,' said Clarissa.

'No harm, love,' said Frank, 'but I'd rather have Kirsten looking after me.'

Bloody typical, thought Clarissa.

Clarissa disappeared to a medical hospital in Edinburgh to have her procedure done, but actually spent two days hiding elsewhere. She returned to the house to begin the charade of her recovery. After two days, she was ready to leave.

'Remember,' said Kirsten, 'you need to be completely different. You need to stay as low key as possible. Wherever you go, don't react. Don't be—'

'Don't be what?' asked Clarissa.

'Macleod's told me about you. Don't be you. Whatever you do, don't react like you. No tartan. Dour.'

'You know what? I'm going to suffer during this.'

'We need to get going. We're going at ten, okay?'

'Fine, I just have to say goodbye to someone,' said Clarissa.

Clarissa walked through her house and out into the garage

where her little green sports car was parked. She stood beside it and put her hand down.

'I'll be back,' she said. She ran her hand across the bonnet.

'I take it that comment was for me.' A pair of arms slipped around her waist, and pulled her tight. Clarissa leaned back and let Frank kiss her.

'Are you okay, Frank?'

'I'm okay,' he said. 'You're scared, though.'

'He wants Kirsten with us at all times. I'm terrified, Frank,' said Clarissa.

'Just go and do, and then get back,' said Frank, 'and trust her to look after you. She's been great these last couple of days with me.'

'I'll be back,' said Clarissa. 'I can't stay away from you two.'

'Who are you going to miss more?' said Frank, and Clarissa turned and smiled at him.

'You can't ask me to choose like that.'

Frank laughed as she stepped forward and hugged him. 'Stay safe,' he said. 'Come back.'

'Of course,' she said. She stepped away. She let her hand continue to hold his until she had to walk through the door. It was time to go. Time to operate in the dark.

Chapter 02

DC Eric Patterson stood at the service station, munching on a Cornish pasty. He'd sat down twenty minutes previously, and now he was up and on the move again. Wearing a pair of jeans, a t-shirt that was hanging out, and an old bomber jacket, he felt scruffy, uncomfortable. Around his neck, he wore a scarf.

It was the only bit he thought didn't look a hundred per cent in character, but he had to cover up the slash across his throat. The scar was an obvious giveaway. In daily life, he wore cravats, but Kirsten had told him not to look like himself.

Patterson had spent a rather pleasant day wandering around a park, waiting for his boss to get down to him and to begin their investigation. He was now sitting in an area next to the car park, which had a food stall serving the Cornish pasties. Watching the cars come and go, he wondered if he would spot them. It wouldn't be difficult to spot Clarissa. The hair, purple or lilac, or whatever other colour she had at this time. The tartan trues, the shawl. Clarissa was a tour de force. Someone who swept into the room and knocked it senseless. Patterson was struggling to see how she would work undercover.

He spotted Kirsten Stewart getting out of a car on the driver's side. Her long black hair was tied up in a ponytail behind her, and she wore a leather jacket and dark jeans. If he was honest with himself, she was quite the looker. But Patterson was also wary of her. She was Service, or ex-Service, at least. And yes, Macleod trusted her. Clarissa said she trusted her. But Patterson didn't know her. Not really. As Kirsten approached him, he saw someone just behind her.

And then his jaw almost dropped. The woman wore a pair of jeans with some trainers and a rather drab-looking Pringle jumper. Her hair was grey, and she wore large glasses, too. It took him a moment, but that was Clarissa.

'You look like you've seen a ghost,' said Clarissa.

'Well, I wouldn't go that far, but they've certainly changed the TV from colour to black and white.'

'That's enough of that, Pats,' said Clarissa.

'Any problems?' asked Kirsten.

'Nope. Ready to go,' said Patterson. 'It was a bit of a walk to get here, though. I'll just get my bag. Stashed it like you said.'

Patterson walked off across the car park, out into the wooded area beyond it. He returned two minutes later with his bag, a hold-all which he had slung over his shoulder. Clarissa had the boot open on the car. It wasn't a little green sports car. It was a rather bland, red hatchback.

'Do you want me to drive?' asked Patterson.

'No,' said Clarissa. 'I'll drive. If anyone's going to do driving around here, it'll be me. I am the best driver.'

Kirsten looked over at her, but then gave a nod. As they set off, further south on the M1, Patterson leaned forward from the rear seats between the two front seats. 'Before we go any further,' he said, 'can I just ask who's in charge?'

'What the hell do you mean who's in charge?' blurted

Clarissa. 'I'm in charge, Detective Inspector, see.'

'Unless it's an operational decision,' said Kirsten.

'No, no,' said Clarissa. 'I'm in charge.'

'When it comes to certain matters,' said Kirsten, 'I'll be the one to say what to do. There are times when I have to make the decisions. You haven't got the experience. The investigation, you can run. But in terms of keeping us alive, that's my call.'

Patterson could see a standoff brewing between the two women, but Clarissa nodded. 'But you run it past me,' she said.

'If there's time,' said Kirsten. 'But when I say something, and the time is short, you have to act.'

'I'm not a little old lady,' said Clarissa.

'Well, that's true,' said Patterson. 'Where are we off to?'

'Oxford,' said Clarissa. 'We're off to meet Kieran Dart. He's an Oxford academic. However, Kieran's had a bit of a rough life. He never achieved the status of professor because he used to make wild assertions regarding certain historical items. What Kieran is, is a man who indulges on the occult side of life. He's into all the myths, the legends, and all the tales. Not sure if he even half-believes some of them, but he's an expert on them and they didn't like that in his world.

'They want you to do the pleasant stuff, the formal stuff, the stuff you can present in front of people who are feeding the university money. Who's going to fund into a lunatic, talking about mystical ceremonies and things like that? But he knows them.

'Kieran works in the university but his existence is more now about finding items from the darker corners of the world. It's one of the things about the art side—certain things are collected from not the best places.'

'How do you even know him?' asked Patterson.

CHAPTER 02

'I know him because I've dealt with people who have gathered the wrong things and not done nice things. This is my world, Pats. Remember? It's not yours. It's not Kirstie's here either.'

'Kirsten,' said Kirsten. 'It's Kirsten.'

'No problem, Kirstie,' said Clarissa. 'He's Patterson, but he's Pats. Okay?'

Kirsten shook her head and then turned to look back out of the windscreen.

'I've contacted him,' said Clarissa. 'Because it's me, he knows we won't meet in the open. However, there's a mound in Oxford, beside the old prison. Up there, in the early hours of the morning is where we'll find him.'

'Why there?' asked Pats.

'It's extremely open. I can see people coming from wherever,' said Kirsten.

'See, Pats, Kirsten's our security expert. This is what she's doing. The artwork, the investigation, the clever bit, that's me.'

The team continued towards Oxford before arriving in the late evening and checking into a hotel. They only had the one room. Kirsten preferred to keep them together, which didn't go down particularly well with Clarissa.

After a few hours' sleep, Clarissa awoke and dressed in the dark clothing she'd brought along. There was a raincoat that she'd bought from a charity shop that ran down to her knees. It had a large pocket though, and the knife that had been recovered by Hope during the previous investigation was placed inside it.

They walked the streets past a few stragglers at one on a Monday morning. It was a student city and never really got to sleep. They soon got to their rendezvous.

The mound did exactly what it said on the tin. It was a hillock with a few trees and a path that ran round circularly, reaching to the very top. Kirsten indicated that Patterson and Clarissa should make their way to the top, and when they looked back again, Kirsten was gone. Clarissa didn't quite stride up, but walked slowly, staring up at the top where she could just about make out a man. It took a bit of puff to get up there. When she arrived, she tried not to wheeze.

Looking back at her was a man of average height. His hair was copiously untidy, and his legs were long. It was dark, but his eyes were penetrating, almost wild.

'You've changed,' he said.

'Kieran,' said Clarissa. 'You doing all right? I thought I saw you pick something up in Egypt recently. Sent out there?'

'That was just for the university. Grabbed some other things, as you do. Not from that auction, though.'

'No, I didn't think so,' said Clarissa.

'You said you had something for me,' said Kieran.

'Were you followed?' asked Clarissa.

'No. But I'm not that happy to meet up here. I mean, it's cold.'

Clarissa had to agree. It was cold, and it was a rather strange place. She was pretty thankful it wasn't raining at the moment.

'Who's the gimp with you?'

'It's just my friend. He looks after me. I'm getting older, you know,' said Clarissa.

Kieran watched Patterson carefully, but Clarissa dug into her pocket and removed the knife. She unwrapped it slowly and then walked forward towards Kieran. 'I need you to look at this. I want to know where it's come from. You see, I can't trace it. It's not normal. It's not—'

The man took it in his hands. He didn't look up at Clarissa once, twisting the knife around and around, then stopping, his fingers tracing along the handle and its carved images. Clarissa could see his shoulders shake.

'Do you know it, Kieran? What is it? Where's it come from?'

He looked up at her, and she could see his eyes were wide in terror. 'No,' he blurted. He dropped the knife where he was and ran, descending the mound. Normally, visitors would go round and round, moving outwards and down along the path. However, Kieran took off and rolled down the steep slope.

'After him, Pats,' said Clarissa. She bent down to pick up the knife, hearing Patterson disappear behind her, then turned and ran as well. She was even slower going down the steep hillock, and by the time she'd only got five feet down, she heard a voice.

'Back up, please.' It was Kirsten. 'We'll do this at the top.'

Clarissa looked to see Patterson was climbing the hill again. Behind him, Kirsten had Kieran by the scruff of the neck, hauling him back up. It was like the hill wasn't there. She was so strong, not even out of breath.

'You,' said Kirsten, throwing the man down at the top of the mound. 'You answer her questions.'

'No. No. Why bring it here? No.'

'What's up, Kieran? What is it? I need to know what it is,' said Clarissa.

'No. You keep that thing away from me. I don't talk about that. I tell nobody about that. We don't talk about it. We say nothing.'

It was almost like the man had gone into a fit. Clarissa held the knife out in front of her.

Kieran backed away until Kirsten stood behind him, forcing

him to stop.

'Certainly seems to upset him,' said Patterson.

'If you two want to step away,' said Kirsten, 'I can exert a little pressure.'

'Get him up,' said Clarissa.

Kirsten hauled Kieran to his feet. As she got close, Clarissa turned, calling Patterson over. 'Hold that a moment,' she said. As soon as the knife was out of her hand, she turned and drove a punch hard into Kieran Dart's stomach. 'I asked you a question,' said Clarissa. 'I want answers. This means a lot.'

Kieran stared at her, his eyes wide. But he said nothing.

'I don't want to do this to you, Kieran, but I need answers. This really means something. This really—'

She turned and drove a punch into his stomach again. The man coughed and then spluttered.

'There's more coming, Kieran. I won't stop. There'll be more coming. You need to give me a start.'

The man looked beggingly at Patterson. He had his head half bowed, as if he wouldn't be worthy to look on his face. Kieran looked back to Clarissa. She was winding her fist back again.

'Amundsen Dig.'

'What about it?' said Clarissa.

'Amundsen Dig.'

Kieran turned away, as if he was expecting another barrage. Clarissa thought for a moment, then turned to Kirsten. 'Let him go.' Kirsten looked at her questioningly.

'I said let him go. Didn't you hear me?' Kirsten released her grip on the man's collar. He turned and fled down the mound. 'You stay quiet,' Clarissa called after him.

'Was that wise?' said Kirsten. 'Letting him go like that? He clearly knows more.'

'He clearly does or is certainly scared of what else he can find out,' agreed Clarissa.

'I could extract it from him. I have been trained to do that,' said Kirsten.

'Kirsten,' said Clarissa. 'Pats here knows me. I have some judgment. We've got what we want. Trust me. Right now, Kirsten. I want my bed. Let's go.'

Patterson looked around for the paper the knife had been wrapped up in and wrapped it again, before Clarissa took it and snuck it inside her raincoat. Kirsten kept a distance, scanning ahead on the streets all the way back to the hotel. Once inside and into the room, Clarissa flung herself down on the large double bed.

'I'll take the sofa bed over there,' said Patterson.

'Looks like you and me are doubling up,' said Kirsten. As the room went dark, Clarissa could hear Pats nod off, a light snore coming from him.

However, the woman behind her in the bed never flinched, and then in the darkness came a voice. 'So I take it you have a line of attack for tomorrow? What to do?'

'Sleep, Kirstie. I'm getting some sleep. I'll tell you where we're going in the morning.'

Chapter 03

Sitting at breakfast the next morning, the small team occupied a table in the far corner of the restaurant. It was half-past eight, just after the busy time, and the more leisurely guests would start to arrive for their breakfast. Clarissa had eaten heartily, and watched in despair at the rather healthier foods Kirsten had eaten. Pats had been himself, a couple of poached eggs on toast, some coffee.

'Now you've consumed everything you've wanted,' said Kirsten, 'do you mind telling me what we're doing today?'

'Amundsen dig,' said Clarissa.

'Yes? Amundsen dig,' said Kirsten. 'I heard that too. What's the Amundsen dig?'

'I don't recall the name Amundsen,' said Patterson. 'I know I'm not as well up on these things, but I have been doing my homework, trying to get on top of the arts world but I've never heard of that name.'

'The name is very minor,' said Clarissa. 'I'm not particularly au fait about anything he did. Certainly not digs. I looked him up on the internet and it doesn't give that much about him. However, not everything is on the internet these days.'

'So what? We haven't really got anything? Are we going back

CHAPTER 03

to Dart? Were you just giving him time to breathe?' asked Kirsten.

'I don't know what they told you, Kirstie, when they did your spy training, but sometimes people pass messages.'

'But you don't know what the message means,' said Kirsten.

'No,' said Clarissa, 'but I'm a detective. He did. Dart was probably bothered that you two were there. You cut a pretty scary figure. I know men say they like the glamorous, all-singing, all-action girl. But when they turn up and grab them by the collar and throw them somewhere, you don't look glamorous. You look scary.'

'Well, now you've complimented me,' said Kirsten; 'are you going to explain how we go on from here, if we're not going back to Dart?'

'I was trying to explain,' said Clarissa. 'Dart wanted out of there. He gave very little; he was clearly scared. In fact, I would say he was petrified, but he knows that I'll come back for him if he doesn't give me something. He's known me in the past. I'm dogged. He saw a side to me there that was even stronger than that.'

'So?' said Patterson.

'So, he wouldn't say it unless he knows I can follow it up. This is him getting rid of me and saying as little as possible.'

'But you're not following it up,' said Kirsten.

'Kirstie, dear, you need to learn a bit of tact. If I'm going to follow it up, it must come from something he's read. The man belongs to the archaeology department here in Oxford. It has a reading room on Beaumont Street. I shall go along there today, get into the reading room, and find out about this Amundsen dig, because . . .'

'Why is it going to be in there?' interrupted Kirsten.

'Because,' said Patterson, 'Dart knows Clarissa knows about the reading room.'

'Been in it with him before, as a guest,' said Clarissa.

'Well, let's hope it's in there then,' said Kirsten. 'Because otherwise, by the time we get round to finding out it isn't, he could have fled the country.'

'He's not fleeing the country,' said Clarissa. 'What he is doing is trying to get me off his back so he can get on with his life as a miserable procurer of things on the fly.'

'Not happy he knows you, though, either. Not with that reaction,' said Kirsten.

'I'm here for the art expertise. Wherever I go, people are going to know me. You need to get that in your head. It's not that big a world.'

'I'll shadow you out to Beaumont Street,' said Kirsten. 'Keep a distance and I'll make sure nobody's following you. After last night, I don't trust you out there on your own.'

Clarissa shrugged her shoulders and half an hour later, was making her way out to Beaumont Street. The street comprised three-storey buildings that almost had a sandstone effect by Clarissa's reckoning. The windows weren't modern, with multiple squares within them. These were also shuttered windows you could throw up or close, with small balconies outside the window that really did nothing for anyone. There were small archway doors, some of them with bright colours like a gaudy blue. And everywhere there were parking restrictions.

Clarissa wasn't a great fan of Oxford, but it had its uses. She found the entrance for the reading rooms on Beaumont Street and engaged the man at the front door.

He took her over to a table, which stood before another door into the reading room.

'And are you faculty?' asked the man.

'Not exactly. Friend of faculty. Kieran Dart.'

'Mr Dart. And your name is?'

'Lorna Green,' said Clarissa.

'Well, Miss Green, or is it Mrs?'

'My marital status is none of your business,' said Clarissa, knowing that a negative response was coming.

'Be that as it may,' said the man. 'I'm afraid Mr Dart has left no word for you to be admitted, and, frankly, unless he's here with you, I can't grant you access.'

'Such an outrage,' said Clarissa. 'I'll be having words with Mr Dart about this. You can expect a complaint.'

'I expect nothing less from you, madam,' said the man.

He was smug, and something inside Clarissa wanted to slap him across his cheek and take him down a peg or two. But she didn't want to make too much of a scene, and so she retired back out to the street. Three corners later, Kirsten appeared on her shoulder.

'That didn't seem to go well,' said Kirsten.

'Won't give me admittance. We'll have to go in there tonight. You able to do that?' said Clarissa.

'Oh, I can get in, all right.'

'You have to take me in with you.'

Kirsten gave a sigh. 'Why?'

'Because you don't have the art world knowledge to find what I'm looking for. Just you and me. We'll keep Pats out of it. Don't want to turn up with too many people.'

'I'll keep him on the street outside. I take it you can run basic undercover as police officers.'

'Patterson's very good,' said Clarissa suddenly. 'Very good.'

'If he was that good,' asked Kirsten, 'how did he get the scar across the neck?'

Clarissa stopped dead. She turned and raised a hand up, grabbing Kirsten's jacket collar. 'Listen, he took a knife across the throat. I held that throat closed, the blood pumping out over my hands. He has seen someone's head shot to pieces in front of him. And he's still here; he's still working. And he came back from awful, awful injuries. Patterson's good. Don't say a word about Pats. Don't think you can't trust him. He'll deliver. You want to think something of me? Fine!' said Clarissa. 'But Pats is salt of the earth. And good with it.'

She let go of Kirsten's collar, turned and walked. She felt a tap on her shoulder and a voice behind her said, 'Fine. But don't do that to me again. You can't back up the bluster. Don't do it. Not with me. Not with anyone.'

'Blusters how I get into most places,' spat Clarissa.

That evening, Clarissa entered the Oxford streets with Kirsten. Patterson followed a little distance behind having been told by Kirsten to make sure no one else was approaching the school of archaeology.

It was fully locked up, dark, thankfully with no students inside. There would be a basic alarm system to contend with. Kirsten approached one of the front doors, picked the lock, and entered. She turned back to Clarissa, dressed in a grey outfit that blended into the dark. There was a beeping from an electronic system, an alarm about to go off. Kirsten saw the panel and attached a device to it. The alarm stopped suddenly.

'What on earth's that?' asked Clarissa.

'My basic alarm system dismantler. It's just something to help me get past simple alarms.'

She tucked her device away and told Clarissa to lead on.

CHAPTER 03

Clarissa made her way past a large oak desk and then into the expansive reading room. There was a gallery around the walls, with many books on the shelves. The ground floor, too, was wall to wall with books. Desks with reading lights occupied the middle of the room. The curtains were closed over the windows. Clarissa turned on one of the lights.

'Switch it off,' said Kirsten.

'You won't see that from outside. Trust me,' said Clarissa. 'I need to see. Right then. Looking for digs.'

'Can I help?' asked Kirsten.

'No,' said Clarissa.

'How long will you be?'

'As long as it takes.'

Clarissa started off searching for general dig-site information. She scanned books quickly, trying to find the name of Amundsen. She found a couple of references, and then after an hour of hunting through other books, she found another reference that led to a small book. It was tucked away up on the gallery and towards the rear of the room.

She brought it down and set it on the desk in front of her. Kirsten looked at it.

'That's barely a notebook.'

'It's exactly what it is; it's a note of digs, Amundsen's digs. It's not a printed book.'

'You're saying this is—'

'These are actual notes from the man,' said Clarissa. 'Amundsen. That's why I'm here, that's why Dart's made me come here. You won't find this anywhere else. It'll be catalogued but it's a nothing book. Nobody will read this, except Dart, except those looking for something from Amundsen. He's been on the trail of something; he's looked at this dagger before or something similar.'

'You don't think he procured it for them?'

'I doubt it. He'd probably be dead by now, wouldn't he?'

Kirsten nodded. 'Good point.'

'Now,' said Clarissa, looking through the book, 'that dig's known.' She whipped into the next page. 'That dig's known, this dig's known, and that one's known; hang on a minute—don't recognise that one.'

'Where is it?' asked Kirsten.

'Heligoland. It's a small island off Germany.'

'I know where Heligoland is,' said Kirsten.

'There's one here that's from Boston I don't recognise. There's another one here in Spain I don't recognise. Give me a minute.' Clarissa made her way back into the books, and brought down a couple more volumes. 'The Spanish one, the American one, are both not well known. Really not well known. Didn't dig up much either. Which is why they're not well known. But they're also not important. Heligoland. That's not mentioned anywhere. At all.'

Kirsten looked at the book. 'These pages around Heligoland have been pulled out more than the others. The book's been laid flat,' said Kirsten. 'Been photocopied. Something like that. What does it show in terms of the dig?'

'Well,' said Clarissa, 'it doesn't say what was dug up. It shows tunnels. It's showing—oh, there's some stones there. But I think some pages are missing.'

'You don't think Dart has them, do you?'

'No,' said Clarissa. 'Dart would leave them in here. Maybe he's found it with them missing. Just a minute.' She made her way over to a desk, reached down, and began looking through some files. 'Book's not registered as being here.'

CHAPTER 03

'So, how did you find it?' asked Kirsten.

'Dart has it in here. It's in the section I would go to but it's not logged as part of that section. Dart has this book that he basically doesn't want to hold in his own house. And he has it here. Either that or he's put it here for me. See? This is him getting me off his back. Like, not wanting me to be around anymore. He's saying, here you go.'

'Does it mean anything, though? Does it give us any detail on the knife? I mean, do we know if the knife even came from there?'

'We know nothing at the moment. Except that Dart ran off after looking at this knife which put him into a cold panic. And he's given me Amundsen's dig site in Heligoland. He's pointing to there.'

There was a sound and the both of them froze. Kirsten reached and switched the light off. The mobile phone in her pocket vibrated. She took it out and looked. *Someone entering*, Patterson's message said.

Kirsten went over to a window, pulled the curtain back, and lifted the window sash up. She then pulled Clarissa over. 'Get out through that window,' she said. Kirsten disappeared out the door, but Clarissa flung her leg up through the window, hauled herself up and basically fell out onto a street. It was only ten more seconds before Kirsten followed her, dropping the window back down, the curtains pulled as best she could before doing so.

Kirsten grabbed Clarissa, hauling her up, and marched her along the street. 'What was it?'

'Somebody entering. I had to activate the alarm again. It's okay. We're out and away. You never said, though, that people come to work here late at night.'

'You never been to university?' asked Clarissa.
Kirsten shook her head.
'Pity. I loved it.'

Chapter 04

'I think we should head to Heligoland now,' said Kirsten. The team were gathered together inside the hotel room where Clarissa had just had a bath. She had one of the hotel dressing gowns wrapped around her over the top of her pyjamas. But even so, Patterson was still looking towards the window, despite the fact the curtains were shut.

'I don't think so,' said Clarissa. 'I don't think it's wise to go yet.'

'Why?' asked Kirsten. 'He's showing you, quite specifically, that he wants you to go to Heligoland. Let's go to Heligoland and find out what's there.'

'Well, one, it's well away from where we are now. It's putting space between us and Dart. Dart clearly knows something. So, to my mind, we need to get that from him,' said Clarissa.

'It seems odd that when he saw the knife, he dropped it and ran,' said Patterson, looking away from the women. 'That's not normal. I've been around these art people enough to know that the one thing they are absolutely obsessed about is their art. If they see something like that, they would hold it, stare at it. They might even try to steal it. These art people—they live for their art.'

'These art people,' said Clarissa slowly. 'Pats, that's not a nice way to put it.'

'Well, you are. You're obsessional. You, Sabine, you're obsessional when it comes to art. The rest of us walk away from it. Not a problem. Emmett didn't have a problem with it.'

'Emmett's not an art person,' spat Clarissa.

'What I'm saying is, if something's scared him, there's a bigger story here he's not telling. And I think we should get the story out of him,' said Patterson.

'Hang on a minute,' said Kirsten. 'You guys were telling me that this is his way of telling you. How's he going to tell you more? He was being stubborn. He wasn't saying anything.'

'What I said was that he was trying to get me to leave him alone,' said Clarissa. 'I'm not going to. I'll go back and get him again.'

'Where?'

'I'll be quite open about it. Do it less clandestine this time,' said Clarissa. 'Maybe I'll go with Pats. We'll just approach him normally. It'll look like we're police officers, not like people approaching in the dark.'

'I don't like that,' said Kirsten. 'I don't like the two of you appearing together in public in front of him, especially if anybody's watching him.'

'Nobody was watching him on the mound, were they?'

'You don't know what he's done since then,' said Kirsten. 'It's always best to mix your people up, yeah? I think we should go to Heligoland and see what the questions are, because then when we come back, you can ask him about what's happened out there.'

'Heligoland is a small place. It's not our territory, is it?

Doesn't that bring problems?' Clarissa said to Kirsten.

'I've operated abroad many's a time. It's not a problem. I can get you in and out.'

'Are you sure? It's not a big place.'

'I appreciate neither of you have ever really seen me in action. But Macleod has me here for a reason. If you don't trust my skills, trust Macleod's decision.'

'I reckon,' said Patterson, 'before we go, we need to know why the knife relates to Heligoland. There's nothing at the moment that relates that knife and Heligoland. All you have is Dart in the middle. He's not telling us why. Did the knife come from there? He hasn't even given any background. He hasn't turned round and said, "Look, this is the link. This is where the stories come from." Or "this is the tale of how it was found." It's just "here's a dig site that doesn't even mention knives." There's just some rocks in the books that you saw. Am I correct?' asked Patterson.

'Spot on, Pats,' said Clarissa. 'We need a better link. It's a heck of a charge all the way over there when we don't understand what it is.'

'But maybe he was telling you to go there for a reason. Maybe he doesn't want you around him. He's scared,' said Kirsten. 'And I did offer to extract the information from him.'

'Well, I say we see him again,' said Clarissa.

'Well, if that's the case,' said Kirsten, 'let me do it. Let me find him first. I want to make sure his habits haven't changed. See what he's doing. He'd normally be found at the university. Yes?'

'He works out of the School of Archaeology,' said Clarissa. 'Should find him there. I think he quite often works down in the basement.'

'Give me the afternoon,' said Kirsten.

That afternoon, Clarissa and Patterson sat in their hotel room, trying to search online and find out anything more they could about Heligoland. It seemed a nice enough place. It had changed hands from being British to Danish to German. The British, at one point, tried to bomb the island out of existence.

There were also tunnels built within. Tunnels were always good. Earlier than that, the Frisians had been in charge back in the more primitive days. Yet, for the life of her, Clarissa couldn't work out a story between the knife and Heligoland.

There were raps at the door, a specified number of knocks that let Clarissa and Patterson know it was Kirsten. She opened the door and entered, but her face wasn't a happy one.

'He's missing. Nobody's seen him. I can't find him anywhere.'

'He'll be in danger then,' said Clarissa, jumping up off her seat. She pulled her mobile out.

'What are you doing?' asked Kirsten.

'I'm calling the local police. To say he's missing.'

'And you're who? You can't be DI Urquhart,' said Kirsten. 'You're having a procedure at home. It gives away you're down here.'

'I'm an anonymous caller.'

'Why? Why is there an anonymous caller saying he's missing? Somebody's down here watching him. No,' said Kirsten. 'Can't phone that in.'

'Well, somebody needs to know. We need to get the police looking for him. We need to—'

'I agree,' said Kirsten. 'But not you. Okay?' Kirsten pulled out her own phone and dialled.

'Hello? Wasn't expecting you to call back this quick,' said

Macleod on the other end.

'Kieran Dart works out of the School of Archaeology here in Oxford. He's missing. Okay? Need you to get contact with local police. Get an English colleague—somebody you know—to call it in. Somebody that possibly would know him. Or get someone to call the Oxford School of Archaeology. Make it known that he's missing somehow. Ask for him. Get them to look for him.'

'Will do,' said Macleod and left the call.

'I'm going to go back out,' said Kirsten; 'see if I can find him. However, you two need to stay here.'

'Great, so we get to sit around and do nothing while you charge off.'

'I am not charging off. I'm also seeing if anybody else is about. At the moment, I think we've gone unnoticed. Understand, one of the greatest dangers to ourselves is getting noticed. And it endangers everybody back up in Inverness. At the moment, nobody knows about this knife except us, Macleod, and the troops up north, and Dart. Dart's a security leak if he goes missing. Dart tells people we've got the knife and it changes things. At the moment people think the previous cases are closed up there; things are going back to normal. It's the way we've got to keep it.'

Clarissa nodded and let Kirsten depart.

'Are you all right?' asked Patterson.

'I got on this arts team and it was my team,' said Clarissa. 'You get that, Pats? My team. You come up with your ideas and you work with me, but I make the decisions. I'm the one that gives the goal and suddenly I've got somebody saying you can't do this, you can't do that. It's not how I operate. I'm the boss of this team and I do what I do.'

'Yes, but you're like a bull in a China shop sometimes,' said Patterson.

'You ever say that outside of this room or in public and I will flatten you!'

'But I wouldn't, would I?' said Patterson. 'I'm telling you what you need to hear. I'm telling you because I'm being honest. You're like a bull in a China shop. Your idea is to rattle feathers, to grab hold of people and shake them. You enjoyed sticking a few punches into Dart. I could see that. In the past, he's done something. He has angered you in some way.'

'The man's a little weasel,' said Clarissa.

'I knew it. I blooming well knew it. Kirsten takes the anger out of it. That's why she's here. She's cool. She's looking at all the other issues that you wouldn't. You just charge after the facts or what you need to know.'

'You're siding with her now,' said Clarissa. 'I take it that's because she looks good. Because she's—'

'Don't you ever say that about me,' said Patterson. 'I owe you my life. I have backed you up as many times as possible. Clarissa, I respect you more than a lot of other people do. Because you have ability. And you are dogged. But don't get grumpy on me. Okay?

'Kirsten's here to protect us. Let her do her job. You've overridden her in terms of going to Heligoland. And I've backed you up because you are right. It's not worth going over unless we know how the knife's involved.

'As soon as we step out into places, we're exposing ourselves. The opportunity to get caught out, the opportunity for others to see we're doing more than we should brings the danger. They could just decide they need to take us out, or they need to take out whoever else back in Inverness. That's the risk we're running,' said Patterson. 'I've nearly died once. I'm not dying again.'

They went silent for a moment and then Clarissa laughed. 'You know what, Pats, I went back to the arts to get away from this stuff and I just charged in on this one. I saw the knife. I saw Macleod needing me and I just went for it. And Frank, God love him, backed me up. And you never hesitated. You went with me. I never realised the danger we're putting ourselves in. At least I never really dwelt on it.'

'You don't, do you?' said Patterson. 'That's why she's here. Why Macleod has made her come along. To protect us. This is not normal. Not normal for any of us.'

'No,' said Clarissa. 'It's not.'

Kirsten returned three hours later. That evening, they found out that Dart had been reported missing, but according to Macleod's contact, there was no great urgency. Dart had done this before, several times, vanishing somewhere, only then to return unharmed. The team had a meal together in the hotel that evening.

'If he's done a runner, why has he done a runner?' asked Kirsten. 'You know the man.'

'I know the man a bit,' said Clarissa.

'Well, he's scared, isn't he?' said Patterson. 'He's clearly scared. He dropped that knife and ran.'

'Who's he scared of?' asked Kirsten. 'Is that how we know the knife is linked? Or at least, is suspected to be linked to the group who we believe carried out Isbister's murder and other ones. People who are controlling agendas, people who are sorting out criminals unethically. So, if it is linked to them, he's seen it and he knows it's linked to them. No wonder he's putting distance between us and him. Does he then go to ground?'

'Macleod said the police noted that he'd done these things before. Disappeared off for a few days.'

'He did. Pats, you're right,' said Clarissa. 'That means he's got somewhere.'

'Do we know where?' asked Kirsten.

'I don't know him that well, only from his art dealings. I know him because he turns up at certain auctions, buys certain types of artefacts,' said Clarissa. 'Sorry, but I don't know where he goes on a Sunday, if he likes the pub, if he likes the park. I don't know him like that.'

'Then we need to find out about him,' said Kirsten.

'So what?' asked Patterson. 'We go ask his friends?'

'Absolutely not.'

'Well, we ask his house then,' said Clarissa.

'Ask his house?' said Patterson.

'We search it. It's what we would do in an investigation. Somebody goes missing, you search their place.'

'But you can't do it openly. Looks like we're going for another nighttime stroll,' said Kirsten.

'It really is a pain, this,' said Clarissa. 'Everything we do, we're doing it under the duvet.'

'Under the duvet,' said Patterson. 'Under the duvet is not an appropriate term. You go under the duvet with a light to hide away from your mum so she doesn't realise that you're looking at your phone at night. You're reading the book; you're listening to music. It is not where you're trying to make sure somebody doesn't come to kill you. Somebody doesn't discover how you're putting the body trail together.'

'Under the duvet,' restated Clarissa. 'So melodramatic at times, Pats.'

Patterson looked at her. 'I'm melodramatic?'

'You both are,' said Kirsten. 'Decision is to search this flat then, yes?'

'Yes,' said Clarissa.

'Right. I'll make plans then. First thing, do we know where it is?'

'I could find that out for you,' said Clarissa.

'From people you trust, really trust.'

'Sabine can get it.'

'No,' said Kirsten. 'Sabine doesn't get involved. Macleod's rules.'

'Right then. Macleod's going to talk to Sam, my new man in Glasgow. He'll get the address for us.'

'Very good,' said Kirsten. 'Let's get some sleep after dinner, then. Looks like we're out tonight.'

Chapter 05

'Remember, no risks. Get in, search, and then we get back out. I'll keep an eye out here, make sure no one comes.'

'You don't think it's my job to give the pep talk,' said Clarissa to Kirsten.

'Not when you're on my territory. This is what I do, so just pay attention.'

Clarissa looked over at Patterson and raised her eyebrows, but she could see the concern in his eyes. It must have been hard for him, for the two women were constantly issuing orders and not working well together. Well, Clarissa didn't like it. She didn't like not being able to just boss the team as she wanted. Especially as this was her team. It was different when she'd come across and worked under Hope. It wasn't easy, but she'd agreed to it.

She hadn't agreed to Kirsten coming in. Macleod had told her. Part of Clarissa thought she could run this herself. But it would be less clandestine. What's the point of being a police officer if you couldn't use the weight of the law? Couldn't get your way in. Maybe she was too old to be running undercover. Maybe she was too old for this full stop. *Nonsense*, she thought.

CHAPTER 05

The fire's still in the belly.

She nodded at Patterson, and together the two of them walked down several streets before spotting Dart's flat at the top of a building. This was the address, the one Sam had discovered. And in truth, Clarissa was intrigued.

She knew Dart in a professional sense. Kieran Dart had a reputation, but most people hearing it would have laughed. He was like some sort of daft professor with all these ideas. All this mumbo-jumbo talk. A man who seemed to take mythology as if it was real. Well, maybe that was just him on the outside.

They approached the front door just as someone was coming out of the flats and gave a nod to them as they entered. The other person gave a quick look but didn't react. Maybe it was the fact that Clarissa was an older woman that made them not bat much of an eyelid.

Without rushing, they made their way up the stairs towards the top flat that belonged to Kieran Dart. Inside would be a picture of Dart. This was his place. How would it be? Clarissa was intrigued. She was intrigued because most collectors who worked in the arts world, they all usually had something kicking about the house that said more about them. They got away from that professional judgement of how much is it worth? How prestigious is it?

Instead, you usually saw what they liked. That was the thing about art. Some of the most beautiful pieces commanded very little money. The art world was distorted, like the real world. True beauty was not always acknowledged, not always sought after. She looked over at Patterson as they stood in front of the door. Was she just becoming too sentimental? She didn't know, but Patterson was pointing at something.

Clarissa looked at the blue door in front of them, and

Patterson was right. Something was up. The door was open. It was barely identifiable because it had swung back towards being closed. There was only a millimetre or two difference between being a shut door and an open one.

Clarissa put her hands up to Patterson, telling him to be quiet, and she pushed the door gently. She stepped in slowly in to see an open-planned flat. She wasn't sure if the design had been like this originally, or if walls had been knocked through, but she could see a living space. There was a kitchen too, quite modern, with a shelf with a number of items on it. And there was a room off to the left-hand side. Another one went off to the right.

Clarissa pushed open the one on the left first and saw a double bed. *'h, he's hopeful*, she thought. And then she looked around. The bedroom was fairly normal, the furniture looking like it must have come from one of those Swedish places with the meatballs. She wouldn't say that out loud to Patterson. No doubt it would be offensive.

She walked further down the corridor to open up the other door, at which point she nearly fell backwards. This was his room. This was his passion.

The room was full of models, knickknacks, trivia, and posters across the wall. Some were incredibly dark. There were several mythologies represented here, there, and everywhere, so much so that Clarissa couldn't keep up with them all. This god, that god. These rituals. These rites. Churches—well, places of worship—images of the afterlife, images of years gone by. There were items in little glass cases on shelves, some of which Clarissa thought looked incredibly impressive.

How expensive they were, she wasn't sure. Clarissa wasn't into the occult or deep into mythologies. Certainly the rather radical ones where they used to sacrifice people. Her art world was different, but this was history, more like historical art.

'Doesn't appear to be anything,' whispered Patterson.

'No,' said Clarissa, 'but somebody's been in here.'

Patterson looked at her, but she pointed up to the shelves as she started going along the items. 'These labels are all wrong. Somebody's been lifting stuff off, having a look, searching under things. These labels have gone back in the wrong place.'

'How can you tell that?'

'I'm no specialist, but those two items are over six hundred years apart. The labels are back to front, and that one, and those over there. Open those drawers on that desk.'

Patterson pulled open the drawer of the desk, and a myriad of papers fell out.

'They've been stuffed in. Somebody's been in here and searched,' said Clarissa.

'Somebody could be keeping an eye on the place.'

'Well, Kirsten's out there. She'll sort us.'

'You've got a lot of trust in Kirstie,' said Clarissa. 'Don't bank on a protector. Don't bank on somebody always saving you, Pats. Gotta look after yourself, too.'

'Well, in that case,' said Patterson, 'we'd better get on searching through this stuff. We don't want to be in here any longer than we have to be.'

Clarissa gave him a look, but he was right. Quickly, the pair started going through the items, Clarissa picking up papers, scanning them. They were full of conspiracy theories, deep examinations into occult practices. It made Clarissa wonder. Did the man know, truly know, what he was on about with the knife? Had he dropped it as a ruse, or did he drop it from sheer fear? Was he now hiding out to get away? Somebody had come and searched, so something was up. Did somebody know about them? Did somebody know they were here?

Clarissa never left the office, continuing to go through, double checking everything. Meanwhile, Patterson went out and swept through the rest of the flat. When he came back in, shaking his head, Clarissa looked up at him.

'I've been through everything here. There's some very interesting stuff, but there's nothing relating to our knife. Nothing relating to Heligoland. If he's got that anywhere, it's not here. Maybe he took it and ran.'

'I don't know,' said Clarissa. She picked up her mobile phone and called Kirsten.

'It's a dead end up here. Can't find anything. Checked his drawers, checked the items he's got. Got a special room full of occult stuff but nothing about Heligoland.'

'Did you find anything untoward?' asked Kirsten.

'Not so far,' said Clarissa. 'Patterson did the bedroom and living area. Nothing in there either.'

'Stay there. I'll be up in a couple of minutes,' said Kirsten.

'She's coming up, apparently,' said Clarissa.

'Why?' asked Patterson.

'Probably doesn't think we did it right. I mean we've searched the places properly. We are the police, after all,' said Clarissa.

It was two minutes later when Kirsten walked into the office area, and Clarissa hadn't heard her at all. The door hadn't even appeared to open, and suddenly Kirsten was there.

'I had a look all over here,' said Clarissa. 'Checked in there,' she said, pointing to the drawer. 'Gone through all the items up. Somebody's been in, though. There are labels that have been switched. We opened the drawer. Papers were everywhere.

Nobody with a mind like Dart, one for information, keeps information like that. They were just stuffed back in. But there's nothing to do with Heligo—'

'Are you sure you've checked everywhere? Thoroughly and specifically?'

'Yes, we've gone through all the places.'

'No, have you checked everything? The walls, the skirting boards, the light switches, the fittings, everything?'

'I saw nothing untoward.'

Kirsten glanced around the room for a moment and her eyes focused on a skirting board just by the desk. She walked up and gave it an almighty kick. Clarissa was stunned when it bounced back off the wall and fell onto the floor.

'Most people with things to hide,' said Kirsten, 'don't hide them here. They hide them away from their usual stuff.'

Patterson looked over at Clarissa, but she ignored him. Instead, she marched forward and put her hands in the hole in the wall that the skirting board had left behind.

'This is more stuff about the dig. It's Heligoland. There's nothing else here. It's all about Heligoland,' said Clarissa. 'It's the place.'

'Is there any more information about it, though?' said Kirsten. 'Is there anything more here than what was in the reading room in that book?'

'Not overly. A few more notes about Heligoland. Some ideas. It's the symbols that were on the knife again.'

'So we have got nothing else? No new information?'

'Not really,' said Clarissa. 'Most of this we knew already, what little there is.'

Patterson had bent down now, and his hands were running along behind the desk. He pulled the desk out from the wall and produced a small note.

'What's that, Pats?'

'This? This is a shopping list,' said Patterson.

'Great, you found his shopping. Well done. Now come on; we need to get back out of here.'

'We haven't found where he is yet, though,' said Kirsten. 'We go over the house again. I'll join you. Make sure we find everything.'

They marched round the house again, Kirsten pulling at switches, delving deep into the back of cupboards to look for false panels. They looked at every skirting board, and Clarissa even gave a couple a kick, only to succeed in stubbing her toe. As they were coming towards the end of a full search round the house, Kirsten shook her head.

'Looks like the trail's going cold,' she said. 'Doesn't appear to be anything here.'

Clarissa looked over. Patterson had the fridge door open.

'Pats, what are you doing? You don't want to take stuff. If you're hungry, we'll get something when you get out of here.'

'Not hungry,' he said. He was holding up the shopping list in front of him.

'What the heck are you doing? We're going to need to go soon. Isn't that right, Kirstie?'

Kirsten rolled her eyes. 'We'll need to go, Patterson.'

'Just a moment,' said Patterson. He held up a finger. 'I'm looking inside the fridge,' he said, nodding his head at the list.

'Come on, Pats,' said Clarissa, getting agitated.

'This is interesting,' said Patterson.

'What?' asked Kirsten.

'The shopping list; it looks fairly recent. None of the items are here in the house. Absolutely none.'

'So it's an old shopping list,' said Clarissa.

'Does the shopping list say anything else?' asked Kirsten.

'Well, according to the date at the top—if it is a date—it's just a couple of numbers, but it would seem to correlate with yesterday. And, says "Water Perry." What's Water Perry? Is that like some sort of funny cider? Perry's a cider, isn't it?' said Patterson.

'You don't get Water Perry. People say it tastes like water, but it's not. Perry's just pear cider,' said Clarissa.

'I've never heard of anything called Water Perry,' said Kirsten.

'Hang on a minute,' said Patterson. He had his phone out, searching for something on the mapping function. He suddenly looked very pleased with himself.

'What is it, Pats? Spit it out,' said Clarissa.

'Near to here, there's a Waterperry Woods, quite an extensive area. That a possibility?'

Clarissa looked at Kirsten, and there was a smile beaming across her face.

'Got him,' said Kirsten. 'Got him.'

Chapter 06

Waterperry Wood was east of Oxford, and Clarissa drove the car towards it. However, she could see in her rearview mirror that Kirsten, in the back seat, wasn't a happy customer. The woman seemed to be almost nervous. Patterson, on the other hand, seemed buoyed by the fact he'd solved something that neither of the two women had managed to do—the whereabouts of Kieran Dart.

'Got a face like a smacked arse,' said Clarissa to Kirsten. 'What's the matter with you, Kirstie?'

'Waterperry Woods is quite large. We don't have an address. There's also been people in his house. They might know it too. They might have found it.'

'I don't know. It was a good catch from Pats.'

'You can't assume there isn't other information there that would have led them that way,' said Kirsten. 'If there is, they would take it with them. They wouldn't leave it. They don't want people knowing that someone was following them if something happens to him.'

'You think something's going to happen to him?' asked Patterson.

CHAPTER 06

'I've done enough sneaking around to know that when people hide things inside skirting boards, when they get nervous just looking at items, something's up. Given the cases that have gone before, I would say we're dealing with people who wouldn't hesitate to kill. I know their type. If they've got quality people working for them, they'd have searched that flat better than you. They may have come up with something. Patterson made a heck of a catch there.'

'So you're just worried about them?' asked Clarissa.

'I'm worried about the fact we have got a whole wood to search, the three of us. Do we split up, or do we stay together?'

'I thought you were here to protect us,' said Patterson.

'I am,' said Kirsten. 'But the objective, at the moment, is Kieran Dart, and he may be in trouble. So, we want to get to him quickly. We'll do that better if we're not all together. I can cover ground quicker than you two can, and much quicker on my own.'

'Why don't you just search the wood then?' said Clarissa. 'Me and Pats will wait in the car and you can just call us.'

'It's too big an area. I wonder how much ahead of us they are. Doesn't take that long to pull a team together, to go and search.'

'You seriously think the man's life's in danger?' asked Patterson.

'Possibly, very possibly,' said Kirsten.

'Then I'll search on my own, and you stay with Clarissa. Why don't you drop me off towards the north?' said Paterson. 'You two can come in from the east.'

'Rubbish,' said Clarissa. 'We'll all go on our own. I might be older than the pair of you but I've a few tricks up my sleeve. I'm not daft.'

45

'Reconnaissance only,' said Kirsten. 'Don't do anything if you see someone. Or if you find a building. Don't go in. Get a hold of me. I'll come. I'll check it out. You stick to the woods. And you stay quiet.'

'If that's the way you want it,' said Clarissa.

'That's the way I want it.'

Clarissa drove and dropped Patterson off at the north side of the woods, then took Kirsten round to the west side before driving the car back to the east. She parked up off the road and prepared herself for a trek through the woods. She put on a black waterproof jacket and some black waterproof trousers, fearing it may rain that night.

Anyway, it would keep the wind off. She donned a black hat and began her escapade into the woods.

It was dark under the tree cover, and Clarissa made slow progress. She decided she really shouldn't take the path that ran through the woods, but that meant going through all the trees. The minor branches tried to catch her face, and a couple of times she went down onto her belly and crawled, an exercise that she hadn't done for many years. However, she didn't see anyone.

A number of times, she stopped, hearing a sound. But the trouble with the woods was the sound could come from so many places. Was it an animal? Was it just the wind? Or was it someone out there? When she stopped, she couldn't see anyone.

She continued on until she saw a small clearing. There was a wooden hut in the dark. *More than a hut*, she thought. *Maybe large enough for a couple of rooms. No lights coming from it. Except, did she just see a flash?*

For a moment, Clarissa went for her phone. No. She'd need

to check and make sure. There was no point bringing Kirsten all the way over here for an empty house. If she got up close, she could look inside and see if anyone was about. She didn't have to go in.

Carefully, Clarissa crept over. There was a window on one side where the curtains were drawn across. She looked up at it and realised that the curtain was just ever so slightly open.

Peering with one eye, she saw a sudden flash of light. It went away again. Slowly, it was replaced by a small flame. Then there was a bit of light in the hut. Not much, just some. Somebody moved across the brief gap in the curtains; then they sat back for a moment, their face suddenly being lit up. It was he; it was Dart.

Clarissa almost trembled with excitement. *This is him*. She should contact Kirsten. She could do it from inside, couldn't she? Yes, that's what she'd do. She'd do it from inside. She'd secure Dart and then Kirsten could come and get them.

She crept along the wall to find the door into the hut. Clarissa put her foot on a step, opened the door quickly, stepped inside and closed it behind her.

Dart was sitting in a chair in front of a small wood burner. He spun almost instantly.

'Hello, Kieran. Don't panic. It's just me.'

'How did you find me?' he blurted.

'You forget I'm a detective. I do more than just look at antiques.'

'The flat was ransacked. Well, it was done well, but it was ransacked. They'd been through everything. That's why I came back out. I've been here for a while to get some things and—'

'Did you get the stuff from inside the skirting board?' asked

Clarissa.

'Yes,' he said. 'I needed to get that out of there. I just went back to check my stuff was okay.'

Clarissa made her way closer over to Dart. 'We were in your flat. I saw it all. You left your shopping list for this place. That's how we found you. Tell me about Heligoland, and the dig? I found the book. Well, the one you intended me to find. But there's not a lot of information about it. Just Heligoland in the dig.'

'I'm not going to tell you. You can punch me again. Do what you want. The thing is, they come for you,' said Dart. 'You need to understand that. They come for you. Once they think you're, well, compromised, they would say. There's a greater good behind it all. You understand that, don't you? There is a greater good.'

'No,' said Clarissa.

'Cleaning places up. Society needs us. Society needs the people who sort out the other people. The ones that normal life doesn't sort out. But they come for you. Can't be discovered.'

'Who comes for you?'

'I'm one of Forseti's,' he said.

'Forseti's? Is that like a colonel or something? Is that the guy in charge?'

Dart laughed. 'You've no idea. Forseti. He's the one. He's helped. It's why it's all . . . it's all been okay. So far. The world gets more turbulent, doesn't it? More turbulent. Gets crazier, but they'll come. They'll come because we can't, we can't, well . . . we can't let people find out.

'You should go. Go. You can't be here. If they come for me and, well . . . they kill me; that'll be it. I don't want you to end up in this. You don't need to be. Leave it all; go back to where you came from. Don't be a detective. Don't—' he reached over now and grabbed Clarissa's hand, pulling it tightly '—don't, whatever you do, don't go further, okay?'

His voice was cracking. Clarissa put a hand on his shoulder.

'Easy,' she said, 'easy; let's get you something to drink. Have you any alcohol?'

The man shook his head. 'There's coffee in the kitchen. It's through there. Not much of a hut, but it's away from everyone,' he said.

Clarissa nodded. True, it may not be much of a hut, but it was certainly well away. She'd heard about hiding in almost plain sight. This was just a hut. It looked like something maybe a trapper or some sort of gamekeeper would have, not the place of an Oxford academic.

But then he wasn't really an Oxford academic. Who was this Forseti guy? Clarissa didn't know the name. She knew all the dealers. She knew many of those who ran cover for them, or who picked up items on the sly. Forseti. It wasn't a name you forgot. Forseti? It wasn't British. Was it European? It didn't sound like it was Southern European.

She entered the kitchen, opened a cupboard, and found a single jar of coffee. She took it down, grabbed the kettle, and went to a bottle of water, for there were no taps and no sink, just a basin. It was a very basic cabin. She saw a flask, however, and went to twist it, when suddenly a hand clamped over her mouth. An arm went around her waist, pulling her back to the far end of the kitchen. It was only a couple of feet extra, but it was taking her away from the door.

Clarissa went to struggle, but the grip was tight. And then she heard a voice in her ear. 'Don't do nothing except what I say. They're all round this place. They're coming for him.

Quiet.'

It was Kirsten. Slowly, she let go.

Clarissa found herself being pulled back. And then her feet found a hole. She disappeared down into it until only her shoulders remained above. Then she looked across and Kirsten was kneeling beside her. The gap was tight, both women barely fitting in. Kirsten put her hand on Clarissa's head and pushed it slowly down below the level of the floor.

There was an almighty bang, and Clarissa thought the front door must have been battered open.

'God no! No!' Dart was crying out. 'I told no one! I told no one! Forseti! I'm for Forseti!'

And then there was silence. No gunshot. Just silence. Clarissa saw Kirsten bend down, so she was below the level of the floor. Quickly, she moved some makeshift floorboards up into the gap above their head. She turned and put a finger over Clarissa's mouth.

It was dark now. Very dark underneath the hut, and Clarissa felt shivers running through her. Kirsten had said they were all over the place. All here.

It felt like an age to Clarissa, but it may only have been ten minutes before Kirsten slowly moved some of the floorboards. She whispered in Clarissa's ear.

'Stay here. Don't move. Don't make a sound.'

Clarissa marvelled at how Kirsten hauled herself back up into the kitchen without a sound being made. She didn't hear her steal across the floor, though she imagined she must have gone to look at Dart.

Kirsten came back about two minutes later, replacing the boards above her. She grabbed Clarissa's head and spoke into her ear.

CHAPTER 06

'Say nothing. I'm saying this quietly. Dart is dead. He's motionless on the floor. There's a needle prick in his neck. It won't take long to heal. The plan would be to leave him here.'

Clarissa simply nodded. She wasn't sure how much Kirsten could see, but the woman still had her hands on Clarissa's head, pulling it closer again so she could speak once more into her ear. 'I will get Patterson. Get him safe, then come back for you. They'll be watching this place at the moment, so don't move from underneath. If necessary, I will eliminate those watching it and get you out.'

Clarissa wanted to say, 'How will you get out in the first place?' but in truth, her heart was thumping. She reached across, as she felt Kirsten's hands leave her head but Kirsten was gone.

Clarissa shook as she sat in the dark. She'd gone into the hut, and if Kirsten hadn't been there, well, then she would have been in trouble. They'd have come in and killed her as well. The realisation wasn't helping.

Kirsten came back, possibly a half hour to an hour later. She led Clarissa under the hut, out another side of it, and quickly took her through the woods. Back at the car, Kirsten told Clarissa to drive.

Clarissa could feel the blood pumping through her veins, the adrenaline still running.

'Everyone okay?' asked Kirsten.

'When did you know?' said Clarissa suddenly. 'When did you know I was in there?'

'I didn't,' said Kirsten. 'I was searching, and I found people searching. One of them got a call on a radio. They were all converging on this hut. I couldn't just run in, and there were too many of them to deal with. So, I found a way into the hut.

My plan initially was to go underneath and listen, to hear what was going on. But I found his escape route.'

'Why didn't he use it?' asked Patterson.

'He said he was one of Forseti's.'

'Who the hell's Forseti?' asked Patterson.

'I don't know, Pats, but he said they would come for him. He was almost resigned to it.'

'And they killed him?' asked Pats.

'They came in and injected him,' said Kirsten, 'left him dead inside. He'll probably be there for days, weeks. There were a couple of them left outside to watch anyone coming back out of the hut or going towards it. They weren't that difficult to get past. I found you, fortunately,' said Kirsten to Patterson, 'because they were sweeping back through the woods. You were on a side that they'd already covered. We got lucky in that sense.'

'Couldn't we have saved him?' asked Clarissa.

'If we'd saved him, this investigation would be over. More than that, you'd have put a target on your back. The smart move was to stay there and let them do their business.'

Patterson glanced over at Clarissa and then glared at Kirsten. 'Just stay there and let them kill him? Couldn't you, like, phone the police or something?'

'Wouldn't have been time. And how's that one work? Who do I say I am? Don't you think they will have contacts for them inside the police? We'd be giving ourselves away. He clearly wanted you to find something out, though.'

'I don't think he wanted us to find something out,' said Clarissa. 'I think he wanted me to be convinced. He said that there had to be an order. There had to be . . . well, Forseti—who the blazes is Forseti?' asked Clarissa.

Chapter 07

'We need to go to Heligoland,' said Clarissa, driving back to the hotel.

'No, we don't, not yet,' said Kirsten.

'Why not?' asked Patterson.

'Because,' said Kirsten, 'we need to know how Dart was found out. We need to know the detail. We need to know if it was us that set it off.'

'No, we need to get ahead of the game,' said Clarissa. 'We need to get to Heligoland first.'

'Do you know anything about Heligoland, Clarissa?' asked Kirsten. 'Small island, small area, quite a bit of water around it. Difficult to get away from. When you go to look at something, when you go to infiltrate, you want to make sure there's plenty of space and plenty of places you can get away to if something goes wrong. We've got no support out there. We're not even in our own country.

'Here, if things go really bad, I've got places I can stash you. I can keep you safe for months, years, if need be. There's the backup of being able to go to Anna Hunt. I might not work for the service anymore, but she'd be on our side with dealing with this. We've got friends here. There are no friends in

Heligoland. There's no one to come and help us.

'If I was going on my own, maybe, but I'd calculate the risk and I'd sure as heck find out what was going on first.'

'Well, you've changed your tune. You wanted us to go there!' said Clarissa.

'But how did they know? They knew Dart had spoken to somebody. They knew he was now a risk. If our names are on that, if it's us, then they'll be looking for us going there. It changes what we have to do to stay undercover. I'm not prepared to take you two when they're looking for us. Not out of the country. Not like that. You're not skilled enough.'

'It's my decision here. My investigation,' said Clarissa.

'It might be,' said Kirsten. 'But it's my choice who I provide protection for. If I'm protecting you over there, I'll decide when we go. Otherwise, you go on your own. But if I'm not taking you, I wouldn't go on your own. You'll end up dead.'

'Wait a minute,' said Patterson. 'Let's all calm down a bit. Things have obviously got a bit heated here. We've just seen somebody killed. Or at least you two heard him die. So, let's just tone it down a bit. What are you talking about doing?' Patterson said to Kirsten. 'What do you think we need to do before we go to Heligoland? Because the plan will be to go. If that's where the answers are, Clarissa's right. We need to go.'

'I don't disagree that your answers will probably be out there,' said Kirsten. 'But first, I want to go back to the flat. I want to search it again. We never got into his electronics. I'll get some devices, see if he's got anything. Laptops, desktops that were kicking about. See if I can find anything on them. I didn't see any devices in the hut.'

'But there were some in the flat, weren't there?' said Patterson.

CHAPTER 07

'Yes, there were,' said Kirsten, 'but I didn't tap into anything in case we left a trace. Usually stuff they leave behind like that isn't important. They'd have taken ones with information away with them.'

'Are you good to go?' asked Clarissa. They had nearly arrived back at the hotel, but Clarissa was now turning the car back into the centre of Oxford.

'I need to get something out of the bag of tricks in the boot. But yes,' said Kirsten.

It was coming close to the early hours of the morning when Clarissa dropped Kirsten off three streets away and then drove off again. She found a place which served breakfast and sat down with Patterson to enjoy some eggs with toast. It wasn't long before Kirsten asked to be picked up and they all returned to the hotel. Once inside the room, Kirsten took a small device and plugged it into a laptop of hers.

'What's that?' asked Patterson.

'It hacks into the laptops, can break into most of the ones that aren't protected very well. Academics are rubbish at protecting their software. Unless they're in that field, which Dart clearly wasn't. Anyway, I'll have all his emails.'

Soon, the emails were on Kirsten's screen. 'I'm going downstairs to get something to eat,' she said. 'Start looking through that. See if you can find anyone.'

Kirsten left the room, and Clarissa sat down to look through the laptop.

'She's something else, isn't she?' said Patterson.

'She's good at her job,' said Clarissa.

'Good at her job. You'd have been dead tonight if it hadn't been for her.'

'And yet, he hasn't sent just her. Macleod wants me, and

he wants you. She's good at her job, Pats, but her job isn't everything. We're needed. And we're darn good at what we do.'

'She's not here, so I'm going to say this,' said Patterson. 'You sound very jealous.'

'Look at her,' said Clarissa. 'She's fighting fit. A strong woman. She's able to do all the fancy stuff. And she's smart enough to hack into things. She's got a mind like Macleod. He told me that before. And she's of an age when she's got all her faculties, and her body isn't falling over itself. Am I jealous? Of course, I'm jealous, Pats. Who wouldn't be jealous?'

'And yet, she's on her own and doesn't truly trust people,' said Patterson.

'What?' said Clarissa.

'She doesn't truly trust people. And she's cold enough to let someone die. You wouldn't be. If she hadn't had snuck you away under there, if she hadn't held you down, and you'd have been on your own, you'd have come back up to save him. Somehow. You'd have gone for Dart. You'd have tried to save him and be dead. There's a piece of her missing. There's a bit of her she has to shut off. She doesn't seem to make connections well. She's standoffish, cold. Especially with you. Though part of that might be you as well.'

Clarissa stared at him. 'I don't need that, Pats, all right? It's intense at the moment. I don't need you being like that.'

'Being like what? I've just told you. The way she is isn't everything. I'm sure your body was that good in its day.'

'It's a very nice thing to say, Pats,' said Clarissa. 'Utter rubbish, but a gracious thing to say.'

'Anyway, you've got Frank. She has got no one, or at least not anymore.'

'What makes you say that?'

'Just something, a hunch. The coolness. I don't know.'

'You know. You might not know the detail, but you know. Not daft, our Pats. It's why you're here.'

They looked deeper into the emails, scanning through. They were reading for about fifteen minutes when Clarissa suddenly pointed at the screen. 'Jennifer Thompson. He tells Jennifer Thompson that something's up. He doesn't say Forseti, but he says, "the one in charge, the one we follow." Look at this, Pats. Have a read of it.'

Clarissa sat back while Patterson read.

'Kieran Dart had written to Jennifer Thompson,' said Patterson. 'He'd said he was going off to the special place.'

'Yes. But had he set that place up on his own, out in the woods? Or had she been part of it?'

'He hasn't even used a dodgy address,' said Patterson. 'It's just her uni address within the archaeology department.'

'There's nothing in it that says anything, if you don't know the other detail,' said Clarissa.

'Yes, but he's written it in the open. They haven't even got a method of communicating that isn't on a public server. It's not private. Yes, it's private within the university, but it's not truly private, if you see what I mean.'

The door opened and Kirsten breezed in. 'You got anything?' she asked.

'He's written to this Jennifer Thompson,' said Patterson.

'Who's she?'

'Undergraduate in the archaeology department. He's put it on this email. It's on her account. It's on her archaeology department account.'

'Okay, Patterson. So, Clarissa, what does that mean?'

'Well, he says nothing in it. He doesn't mention Forseti. But he talks about the special place, which must be the place in the woods, says he's going away, says that something's up, that people are onto it. He mentions people.'

'Does he mention us by name? Or does he mention any description of us?' asked Kirsten.

'No, not at all,' said Patterson.

'Move off the seat a minute,' said Kirsten. She slid onto the seat, quickly vacated by Clarissa, and started tapping into the laptop. It took her two minutes before her face became gravely concerned.

'I'm not the only one that's been into this. Hell, we need to find Jennifer Thompson, and fast.'

Clarissa picked up her phone and called the archaeology department, looking for where Jennifer Thompson would be. A woman on the end of the phone advised that she'd be attending a lecture within the archaeology department. Within minutes, the team were in the car on Beaumont Street awaiting Jennifer Thompson to exit from the department.

'What's she look like?' asked Kirsten. 'Anyone know?'

Patterson held up his phone. 'She's on the website, undergraduate photos, that's her.'

Jennifer Thompson was diminutive, with her long, black hair. She was thin, quite small and narrow, if the image was anything to go by. The woman was standing in a group photograph, but she seemed to have quite thin legs. She was wearing a skirt, but it only came down to her knee.

'Drainpipes for legs, hadn't she?' said Clarissa.

'Get her face in your head,' said Kirsten. 'Out of the car; everybody surround all the areas that they can leave this department from. Shout when you see her.'

CHAPTER 07

It was half an hour before Patterson called and said she was leaving by the rear entrance. He was following her along the street and Kirsten tagged into Patterson's phone to see where he was going. She rendezvoused with Clarissa at the car and then Patterson called again to say the woman was getting a bus.

Clarissa drove the car until they found the bus, at which point Patterson got off, joined the car and they continued to tail it. It stopped by a cemetery called Rose Hill, and Clarissa parked the car up in a nearby street, while Kirsten tailed Jennifer Thompson.

Clarissa remained on the outside of the cemetery before making her way over to a side entrance, where she rendezvoused with Patterson. Kirsten soon joined them.

'She's gone off to a grave. Seems to be talking to it. We'll keep our distance at the moment. This may be a rendezvous, but she could also be just visiting a grave of someone. Who knows? I'll check it in case she's dropping something off. That happens sometimes. The two of you keep a distance. Go together to a grave—somewhere where you can see me. Okay?'

Kirsten made her way quietly amongst the graves and then stood before one, able to see Jennifer Thompson. The woman was standing in a raincoat and her legs were indeed like drainpipes, as Clarissa had commented. But the woman looked edgy. A car arrived at the graveyard. Jennifer Thompson was now on her knees in front of the grave, and Kirsten bent down in front of the one she was at.

She was over two yards away, not wanting to be close, and she saw two men get out of the car. They were moving quickly towards Jennifer, who didn't even look round at them. It was almost as if she was in prayer.

No, thought Kirsten. She thought about Kieran Dart. He had accepted his fate, waited for them to come for him. Wrapping her scarf about her face, she broke into a run, but the men were now close to Jennifer Thompson. One of them arrived at Jennifer and produced a needle while the other man looked over towards Kirsten coming towards him. The first man drove the needle into the side of Jennifer's neck while the other ran towards Kirsten. He produced a nightstick from within his coat.

Kirsten dodged the initial swing, landed a punch on his shoulder, but the man hardly flinched. He rained punches towards her, and she ducked this way and that. He was good; very good. A punch caught her across the temple, making her head ring, but she rallied, spinning and driving an elbow up into his face. The other man shouted at him and Kirsten kicked out while the man was momentarily distracted. He tumbled backwards, but rolled and ran. Kirsten went to run towards Jennifer, but the woman suddenly pitched forward, face driving straight into the grave in front of her. The body lay prone.

Kirsten turned back to the car, shouting at it loudly in German. The car sped off. Kirsten ran after it, but then realised she would not get close.

She turned to see Patterson and Clarissa running towards her. Clarissa put her hands up, waving at them, pointing back to the other exit. As Patterson reached her, she said, 'Out of here, now. Don't say a word, both of you go to the car. Just to the car. Let's go.'

'But is she—?' asked Patterson.

'She'll be dead. Go.'

Without hesitation, Patterson turned. Clarissa was swept

along with the pair of them as they raced back to the car. As she jumped into the passenger seat, Kirsten turned to Clarissa.

'Any direction away from here! Just go!'

Quickly, they drove off. As soon as they were little more than a half a mile away, Kirsten put her hand across to the steering wheel.

'Easy. Slow. Just drive away normally. Head off to the motorway. We'll drive a couple of miles up. We'll stop at a services. I'll just check we're not being followed. If we're not, we'll head back to the hotel.'

There was silence for a moment. And then Clarissa spat, 'Did they see you?'

'I'm sorry?'

'Did they see you?'

'No. I had my face covered. That first guy, though. That guy's a professional. He could fight.'

'What about the second one?' said Patterson.

'I didn't engage him, but they were delivering an injection that kills. He must have known where to put it.'

'They'll know somebody's on to them, though, won't they?' said Clarissa. 'Our cover will be blown. They'll suspect it's us. They'll suspect Macleod. We're the only path for them to think of?'

'I spoke in German at them,' said Kirsten.

'German?' said Clarissa. 'Why?'

'Heligoland's just off Germany. They know about Heligoland. They'll know about the site. Somebody's been in. Somebody knows from Dart about the site. Why wouldn't it be German authorities? If there's something to protect in Heligoland, why wouldn't it be German authorities? Hopefully, it'll keep them off our tail.'

Clarissa nodded and continued along in the car, but something inside her said Kirsten wasn't that convinced. And Kirsten, not being convinced of their cover, worried Clarissa.

Chapter 08

Macleod looked out of the window as his plane touched down at Gatwick. They'd come in through some low cloud, so the arrival of the runway was quite sudden. Macleod sat back, his hands almost instinctively going out to the armchair rests, bracing himself for the inevitable heavy braking by the pilot to turn off at an early exit.

He was on his way to Brighton for a conference, something about maintaining relationships in today's modern policing. Macleod hadn't been intending to go. But having seen it was on and also knowing that at some point he had to attend some conferences to keep up his quota of CPD, he decided on this one. After all, Brighton wouldn't be that far away from the team.

Once off the plane, Macleod took the little monorail across to the South Terminal and caught a train heading for Brighton. Before he got on, he'd scanned up and down, checked who was on the surrounding platform, had watched when he'd walked through Gatwick if anyone was tailing him.

But there was no one. No one at all. That being so, he sat back, trying to relax as his train departed for Brighton.

'The Sanderley Hotel,' said a voice. Kirsten was in the seat behind him, whispering through the gap. He watched as she sauntered off down through the train coach. She passed him by again three minutes later, giving him a nod, just to make sure he had got the message. It was ten minutes later when he looked round and saw she'd taken a position up at the rear of the coach.

She was watching him down to Brighton. Maybe she'd been in Gatwick as well. He'd got a message previously saying they needed to speak to him, and he told them that there was a conference in Brighton. After that, he hadn't spoken, and yet, here was Kirsten with him, and keeping an eye on him.

Macleod could book just about whatever hotel he wanted, although he had to indicate most of them in advance. He, however, had said that he had a slight detour to make, and therefore would pick up a hotel on arrival. What he had wanted was for the hotel to be picked out by Kirsten, so he knew it was safe, and he knew they were close by. Arriving in Brighton, he caught a taxi for the Sanderley, and on arrival, announced himself to the receptionist.

'Ah yes, Detective Chief Inspector Macleod, isn't it? I believe you're booked in for the conference that's happening.'

'That's correct,' said Macleod.

'Here's your keys,' said the woman. 'It's three floors up. Got a delightful view of the city.'

Macleod thanked her, got into the lift before getting out on the third floor and turning down two corridors to find his room. As he arrived, he thought he could hear something inside. Macleod touched the keycard to the pad, heard the barrel revolving away from the lock and pushed open the door.

CHAPTER 08

'Get inside, will you?' said Clarissa.

Macleod was a little unsettled. Why were they here already? And how did they get into his room? He'd only just checked in.

Kirsten was sitting in the far corner on a chair, and he could hear the kettle boiling.

'It's going to be instant,' said Kirsten. 'But I thought you could do with one.'

'Absolutely,' he said. 'I take it I'm the only one sleeping in here, though.'

'Totally,' said Clarissa. 'As if you'd be lucky enough to have me in your room.'

Macleod gave her a quizzical look. He was a little worried, though. She was making quick puns. Quick jokes that were more than the usual. She was worried. Clarissa didn't show worry. She either told you, quite forcefully, or she hid it, if she didn't think it was worth bringing up. If she didn't think this was worth bringing up, Macleod was really worried, because that meant she'd decided, and she wasn't bothered about discussing it.

'Where are we at, then?' asked Macleod.

Clarissa ran through all that had happened, everything about Kieran Dart and Jennifer Thompson, and their deaths.

'Because of what's in the notebook, and because of what we found, and because they seemed to dispatch them, we need to go to Heligoland.'

Macleod sipped his coffee, but he could feel his chest beginning to pound.

'Heligoland, little island just off Germany,' said Macleod. 'You're out of the UK, you'll be beyond any protection that Anna Hunt has got in place.'

'She hasn't got any,' said Kirsten. 'I think she's looking after your end, not ours.'

'And,' said Macleod, 'you're on foreign soil. Last time two of my officers were on foreign soil, somebody took a pot shot at them. I'm not keen on this. We go outside the UK and things could turn nasty.'

'Nasty,' said Clarissa. He felt she wanted to raise her voice, but was maintaining a lower volume so as not to be heard. 'How nasty do you want it to get, Seoras? There's two dead. Two people dead.'

'Well, if that's where the trail's leading, I guess you'd better check it out. Do you want me to do anything? Make any arrangements?' he asked Kirsten.

'I'm still running the investigation,' said Clarissa.

'Yes,' said Macleod. 'But with all due respect—'

'Don't "due respect" me!'

'Okay. To state the bleeding obvious,' said Macleod, 'Kirsten has worked overseas. Kirsten knows how to get you there. Kirsten knows how to look after you. So, I'm talking to Kirsten when I'm asking if she needs any help.'

Clarissa almost grumbled, but she gave a nod, showing he was right. Instead, she turned, grabbed some hotel paper, and pulled out a pen. She began writing and showed no sign of stopping for anything Macleod was going to say. So, he turned back to Kirsten.

'I'll make the arrangements,' said Kirsten. 'Better if I do it completely. No involvement from your end. In fact, once we're done here, we're gone. Out of this hotel. You're back on your own.'

'Should I be worried?' asked Macleod.

'I don't think so. If somebody was after you specifically,

CHAPTER 08

Anna Hunt would organise protection,' said Kirsten. 'She's very fond of you.'

Macleod raised an eyebrow. 'I keep hearing this. Obviously, the woman's idea of "fond" is different from mine.'

Patterson almost laughed, but Macleod looked over at him, staring for a moment.

'Are you good, Patterson?' he asked. 'If it's too much, you can drop out.'

He shook his head. Macleod returned to his coffee.

There was something else on his mind, something he wanted to get back up the road to. And it had come at an inopportune moment. It was just that morning when she'd said it to him.

'Are you okay?' asked Clarissa, finishing her note. 'You don't look yourself, Seoras.'

'You mean, beyond my team running around with two people killed in front of them.'

'It's not about us,' said Clarissa. 'What's wrong?'

'My secretary has just been diagnosed with cancer,' said Macleod. 'She told me this morning. I sent her off.'

'Sent her off?' said Clarissa.

'Told her to take whatever time she needed. I'm not sure she'll be coming back.'

'You mean she won't make it? Is it terminal?'

'It's not at that stage,' said Macleod, 'but she's not, well, let's say she's got a bit of a fight in front of her. And if she gets out the other side of that, she doesn't want to be stuck at a desk looking after me.'

'You going to cope all right?' asked Clarissa. 'She was picking up most of that paperwork, organising it for you. You're not, well—'

'Not what?' said Macleod.

'You used to have Ross. Ross used to organise everything,' said Patterson suddenly. Macleod frowned. 'Well, Clarissa told me. Hope told me that too. Ross never did. Ross organised you, though. That's what they said.'

'One thing I don't like about this first name thing is that everybody just opens their mouth and doesn't actually know when not to say something,' said Macleod.

He saw Patterson go red, almost blushing.

But Clarissa blurted in. 'Well, he's absolutely right.'

'I know he's right,' said Macleod. 'And I know I need a decent secretary, someone to sort me. But, I was wondering at the moment, should I be looking for more than a secretary?' He looked over at Kirsten. 'I'm worried if I get someone in now, they could be a plant. Perfect opportunity to compromise me.'

'Maybe you should look for more than a secretary,' said Kirsten.

'Because?' asked Macleod.

'Because these people are moving about far too easily. It's like the Service. They seem to have enough resources too. This will worry Anna. You don't get many people that move like the Service in the UK. So many places you can turn to as the Service. So many options to call on. These people react far too quickly. Far too effectively. That's why I'm going to go dark. I'll contact you if I need you. But otherwise, Heligoland becomes the last you'll know. At least until we come back.'

'What if I discover something else?' asked Macleod.

'I'm not going that long. I can't keep Clarissa recovering for too long. Patterson's got to come back from a holiday at some point.'

'Trust me, it's not really a holiday,' said Patterson.

'Look,' said Macleod, 'because you're about to go away,

because you're about to step outside the country, because you're about to step outside the bounds of what you really should do, and if you get caught, I don't know how much we can own up to, I want to ask you all, are you happy to go ahead?'

'You know my answer,' said Kirsten. 'I wouldn't be planning it at all if I wasn't happy. You'd be told.'

Macleod nodded and gave a faint smile. 'Patterson?'

'I'm good,' he said. 'I need to see this through. But I don't like this.'

'What about my Rottweiler?' asked Macleod. Clarissa gave him a look. But then she softened somewhat.

'I have to admit, I'm scared. Seoras, I'm terrified. For all of us. As much as Kirsten knows what she's doing, this differs greatly from what I signed up for.'

'Well, you can call it,' said Macleod, 'any of you. You can call it and walk away. I wasn't expecting it to be this rough. I was expecting a hunt for a knife,' said Macleod. 'I was expecting you to do it without attracting too much attention. But clearly these people look at things much closer than I would have thought.'

'They killed one of ours,' said Clarissa suddenly. 'They killed Gavin Isbister. They've killed other people. No doubt, some of them may be even deserving of it. But it's not right. I may charge in a little heavy,' said Clarissa, causing Pats to look over and raise his eyebrow. 'Yes, Pats, this is true. I have my own way. I may have gone outside the law at times to save people.' At this she looked at Macleod. 'I can also get that our friend here in the corner has done some things to protect the national interest, but she is under the rule of someone that we trust for that.

'But,' said Clarissa, 'these people, they seem to be arbiters of their own truth. Whatever happens, they're going to close ranks. Then they killed one of ours to do it. I'm a police officer. I can't look away from that.'

'Okay,' said Macleod. 'But remember, if it gets too much, you can call it quits and come back.'

'But if I do that, you'll just jump out here,' said Clarissa. 'You won't do it at the moment, because you say it's not worth the risk, or the risks are too great. You'll be identified too easily. There's no way I'm going to let you do that.'

'Agreed then,' said Kirsten. 'I'll get it under way.'

As everyone got up to leave, Macleod wished them the best. But while Clarissa and Patterson went through the door to exit the room, Kirsten hung back.

'If you're looking for a new secretary, don't advertise. Not at this moment in time,' she said. 'Find someone. Put them on a trial basis. But find someone we know, you know, or somebody you trust knows. Probably best if you don't know them, but they come from a reliable source. That would be the best thing.'

'I don't know if I can do that. I'm quite fussy,' said Macleod. 'I need somebody that understands me. Somebody that can—'

Kirsten took him by the shoulders. 'Right now, you need someone you can trust. And someone who's astute. Someone who knows the lay of the land around you. Prepared to take action if needed. You don't necessarily need someone like me,' said Kirsten. 'Just someone who's prepared to be on their toes, look out, and get someone like me if needed. You don't need a friend; you need a good colleague, one who's going to look out for you. We'll be back shortly,' said Kirsten. 'It won't be a long trip to Heligoland, but I think the answer's out there. How much the answer will help in finding these people is another matter but something's out there.'

'How's she holding up?' Macleod asked Kirsten.

'The Rottweiler? She's doing okay. But it's a bit like you in Italy.'

'What do you mean?'

'You walked into my territory. You didn't even give a "What should I do? How do I do this?" And then were shocked when I stepped across you and saved your backside. Both of you have far too much confidence when you don't know the lay of the land. Doing your own jobs, fine. My job is different.'

Macleod gave a nod. 'True,' he said. 'Take care of her. But if it comes to the detective work, if it comes to seeing what's underneath this, trust me, she's one of the best. She'll find it, especially on the art side. She's worth the hassle.'

'We'll see,' said Kirsten. 'Look after yourself.'

And with that, she was out of the door. Macleod went downstairs and had a coffee in the hotel, looking out his front windows onto the street before him. He had two days of this conference coming up and not a single bit of interest in it. His thoughts were on Heligoland. How on earth did a small island off Germany fit into all of this? He shook his head.

It was getting more and more strange by the minute.

Chapter 09

Clarissa had tied a scarf around her head to keep her currently grey hair packed down tight. The ferry over from Germany cut through a bright spring day, but delivered a blast of cool air to their cheeks.

Clarissa's were turning rosy red as she leaned over the side, watching Heligoland get closer. Its large rock faces meant the island looked as if it had been lifted, carved to have a flat top, placed rather than worn out. From the aft of the vessel, as it spun round to dock, Clarissa could see plenty of hotels and cafes.

'The museum's further up to the north of the island. Not much of a walk though,' she said.

'No, it's not,' said Kirsten, whispering in her ear. 'It's also close quarters for us all the time. If somebody's here to watch us, they don't have far to travel. There may be a number of them. Possibly people who don't even know what we look like, searching for whoever's coming. They'll have an idea somebody's coming. The records have been disturbed, and therefore, they've killed off Jennifer Thompson and Kieran Dart. Eyes open!'

'What do we do when we arrive?' asked Patterson.

'Well, the first thing we do is find our apartment. Then we're going to walk. Remember, we're meant to look like tourists,' said Kirsten. 'Brother and sister taking their old mum on holiday.'

Clarissa gave her a look. 'So you enjoy yourself, Mother.'

'The notes from the dig show we should look up near the museum. So, we'll start there.'

'No,' said Kirsten. 'We'll take a walk round the island first. Then we'll go to the museum. And we'll look as if we've stumbled upon it. Not like we're going there directly.'

Clarissa nodded again. 'Is this me meant to be the older woman, getting told by the younger people what to do? You're certainly getting into character,' she said.

'Macleod makes less noise than this,' said Kirsten in a hushed tone.

She walked away to the other side of the boat, leaving Clarissa looking out along the island with Patterson.

'You know what, Pats? She'll grate on you after a while. Thinks she knows it all. Thinks she's got more of an idea than you have.'

'I have no idea what that would be like,' said Patterson. Clarissa turned, but the man's face was expressionless. 'Lovely island, though, isn't it?' he said.

'Beautiful,' muttered Clarissa.

Leaving the ferry, Clarissa had her arm taken by Patterson. She feigned slight difficulty in walking and Patterson supported her. She was happy enough playing the part, except for how Patterson said, 'Come along now, Mother,' constantly hanging on the word 'mother' as if to annoy her.

They made for their apartment, obtained the keys, and unpacked inside. Only then did they walk round the island.

Clarissa bought a couple of minor items, and they stopped for coffee, before making their way further round and then towards the museum.

'Do we want a guidebook as we go in here? Get us a guidebook. Be good to your mother,' said Clarissa.

Kirsten disappeared off and came back with one as they came to the museum. Just outside of it were what almost looked like beach huts. Old style, wooden, bright colours on them. And just beyond were the tickets to get entry to the museum and the bunkers.

Clarissa was deep into the guidebook. 'Do you know what it says here? This used to be a place for bathing. It had like carts that would take you down. So, two wheels and completely open on the sea side. Horses pulling them in and out, or else some poor people dragging them. Apparently, they used to have four-wheeled models. They were sturdier because the weather was rough. People took to this bathing to try and increase their circulation.'

'You should go and do some bathing,' said Patterson. 'Be good for you, Mother.'

Clarissa glared at him. They continued to look round the museum and Patterson was deep in a book when Clarissa came up on him.

'What's that about?' she asked.

'Interesting, talking about some dig sites up here. You know there was quite a number, not just here but all round northern Europe. Poems and stuff about giants, references to incantations. There's a lot of stuff here that's quite different. There are also ritual offerings. All about times before Christianity came to the islands and different places.'

'It's one of the troubles you've got,' said Clarissa. 'Everybody sees it through modern-day lenses. Got to look back to a time before there was Christianity when people were looking with more suspicion at the world, or saw gods and different things. Some of the items you find may not be mystical themselves, but they were mystical to the people who were there. You get apocryphal stories, mythical stories, lots of different things. I don't know what we'll get here, though.'

They continued to wander round.

'This place was bombed during the war,' said Kirsten, 'because of the island's military use. It was one of the largest explosions in world history. Thousands of tons of ammunition. It's quite a unique complex, but it's very modern. I'm not sure how it's going to work in with what we're looking for.'

'According to the dig information, it was up here on this part of the island,' said Clarissa. 'But what I don't understand is the dig site that is stated in the book from the reading room, well, it would have been in amongst the tunnels. Tunnels would have gone through it. This dig site can't exist anymore. I mean, we are talking about it being dug out one hundred and fifty years ago—more than that possibly—so it's well before anything was brought into the Second World War.'

'There were almost fourteen kilometres of these underground bunkers.'

'That's amazing, isn't it?' said Patterson.

'Well, there's not fourteen kilometres in what we're seeing,' said Kirsten. 'I wonder how much of it still remains. I wonder how much of it—well, do we get to see everything?' The group took a tour of the tunnels. In some ways, they were incredibly simple. Yes, now they were lined with lighted information boards that told of Hitler and other information about World War II, lit up by subtle lighting on a grainy floor.

The tunnel in the tour was only two hundred metres long though. In order to visit them, they'd had to take a guided tour, and they stood together as a three, listening to the history.

The island had been an incredible sea fortress, but all Clarissa could think of was what had happened to the dig site when they made these tunnels. There weren't a lot of tunnels here. This was small, and there had been fourteen kilometres underneath. Had the dig site been brought out then? Had it been destroyed? What was the point? What had Dart known, his secret about the knife? Did the knife come from here? Who did it represent?

There was nothing in the tunnels to say about the real history—the long-ago history. To Clarissa, the knife seemed to be an old one. A really old one.

'Pack up. Let's go,' said Clarissa once the tour had been done.

'Do we not want to look elsewhere? Isn't there anything else you want to see? Anything sparking something?' said Kirsten.

'No,' said Clarissa. 'This is all wrong. This is all modern history. World War II. We need to look beyond that, need to look at what happened to the dig site. We need the local records. They'll have local records here somewhere.'

'Why don't I look for that?' said Patterson.

'Why?' asked Kirsten. 'Why you?'

'I'm trained up enough on the detective side of things to do it. Clarissa pitching up won't look right. She's the old mother walking about. And what? Runs in looking for records? I can go in looking like the most boring man ever. Oh, I can do that. I can be the bland one. Somehow, I don't think you'd cut it at boring,' he said, turning to Kirsten.

'He's always this charming,' said Clarissa. 'It's one of his faults.'

CHAPTER 09

'But he's right,' said Kirsten. 'We'll do that. We'll check the records, and we'll stay here. Not just disappear because if we do that, it'll look bad. We want people to think we're here for the duration. Like we're here, enjoying ourselves. I'll find us a restaurant for tonight. We'll take you out, Mother. Live it up a bit.'

The team made their way back to the apartment before Kirsten disappeared. Clarissa suspected she was doing more than just finding a restaurant. She would scout the place, see if anyone was watching. As Clarissa sat in the apartment, she could feel herself beginning to shake. She hadn't done this before, being out in the open so much. She saw Pats looking at her.

'What's up?' she said to him.

'You okay?' he asked.

'Don't you feel a bit exposed?'

'Yes,' said Patterson. 'Very much so. But we need to rely on her. She'll know if we're really exposed.'

'Not used to that. I know my territory back home, know what I'm doing. I know where the bad people are. Here, I'm looking around and I don't even understand the language most people are speaking. I'm not comfortable, Pats.'

'You must have been abroad before, working in the arts field.'

'Many times, but I was younger,' said Clarissa. 'You've got to remember that, Pats. You're still in your youth, still in the flush of being a detective. Not me. I've done this too long. Seen things that can go wrong. I like the comfort of knowing what's around me. I don't take on the new things well. Having to get on with her. Having to come out here. I'm not on a sure footing.'

'We'll be fine,' said Patterson. 'Just go with it. You're doing okay.'

'If you say so,' said Clarissa.

That wasn't a Patterson statement, she thought. That wasn't for me, the boss. He's always giving little digs to get back at me for being too overconfident, for being the one pushing. I'm not pushing at the moment.

Kirsten came back about an hour later, and the three of them dressed for dinner. Their clothes were modest, but certainly smarter than they'd been while they were wandering round. They didn't have a large amount of clothing with them, but they had options, as well as packing items that would help them be disguised.

There was a lot of reversible clothing, black on the inside. You would only notice if you turned the clothes inside out, and even then, it was just the fashion, wasn't it?

The restaurant that night had a view off the shores of Heligoland, and Germany was in the distance. It was quite beautiful, if a little nippy.

Once inside, Clarissa enjoyed a couple of drinks. In truth, she needed the alcohol to steady herself. Damn, she needed to relax. She was at her best when she was in the flow, at her best when she was appreciating what was about her. And there was plenty of history here. Yes, it wasn't quite what they were looking for, but it was all history, all tales of the past.

Some items from World War II in the museum had been deeply interesting. It wasn't quite art, but they were artefacts, most of them, albeit modern.

A fish course arrived. Clarissa hungrily dug into it, but she saw Kirsten looking this way and that. She excused herself at one point, disappearing off to the bathroom, then came back again. And at one point, Kirsten moved her chair round, as if she wanted to talk more closely to Clarissa.

'In two minutes, get up and go to the toilet,' she said. 'When you do, at the table behind you, you'll see a man. Don't watch him too closely, but take a glance. Remember his face.'

'Why?' asked Clarissa.

'Because he's watching for someone. He's not watching for us, or maybe he is, but just doesn't know what we look like. But he's been watching the whole time. It's subtle, but he's not that good. The problem for observers is that they have to look, and that gets noticed.'

Clarissa stood up, made her way out to the bathroom, glancing round just the once to look at the man. On the way back in, she glanced at him again. But when she sat down, she turned to Kirsten. 'Seriously, is he really looking for someone?'

'Completely,' she said.

'Are you going to follow him, then?' asked Clarissa.

'Definitely not. We're going to let Patterson go tomorrow and check the records. You and I are going to sightsee. We are going to be tourists. The last thing I'm going to do is go near that guy or give him any reasons to suspect us. He clearly doesn't know who we are, so the best way to remain undetected is in the open and being what we're not.'

'Very good,' said Clarissa, but underneath, she had held one hand in the other because it was starting to shake. People were watching for them. What happened if they found them? How did you get out of here? How did you leave? If you were undetected, it wouldn't be a problem—get back on the ferry, and off you go. But if they were spotted, if they were suspected . . .

'Calm yourself. Calm yourself,' Clarissa said to herself. 'You're with a professional.' *Yes*, she thought. *That's right, that's better. I'm with a professional.*

The trouble was for Clarissa, she found it hard to lie to herself. On the way out of the restaurant, she checked the man over once again. She wouldn't have known. Never have clocked it. But Kirsten had. And if Kirsten wasn't with her, would Clarissa be safe?

Clarissa wasn't here for her ability to run around and sneak by. She was here for her expertise. Part of her wished Kirsten could bring stuff back to the UK for Clarissa's expertise to be used there.

As she walked back to the apartment, she thought of Pats the next day. He'd be out there alone. She suddenly wondered where her confidence had been.

'Come on,' she told herself. 'This is you. You're more than this. You're the Rottweiler. Time to bare some teeth.'

Chapter 10

Patterson stepped out of the apartment into a day that was brimming with brightness. Heligoland was quite the place. Small, yes. A tiny island sat on the edge of Europe, or at least on the edge of Germany. Maybe he was being overdramatic. Maybe working with Clarissa was what did that. Either way, he had a job to do, but he was going to enjoy the surrounding scenery.

Everywhere was immaculate. The hotels, the buildings, the restaurants. Maybe it was being in such a small place that did it. He could see the ferries that came and went across what was today a crystal-blue sea. But one thing that Patterson was enjoying was the fact he was going off to do this on his own.

Often with Clarissa, he was working alongside her, but every now and again he got to do something himself. Today would be fun. He'd be acting. He reached up and adjusted his cravat. There was one thing he struggled with. The scar that had been left from where his throat had been slashed made undercover work difficult. While when he was on the arts team, he could march about wearing a very lush and stylish cravat. For now, he was wearing a modest and plain cravat, in line with the shirt he had on.

He had a small rucksack over his shoulder with a little notebook, as if he was a tourist for historical things. To begin, he started off back at the tunnels and the museum of Heligoland. He asked there about dig sites in general, knowing that he would get very little information. They looked at him, almost a little surprised.

'Digs,' he said. 'Archaeological digs. Do you understand?' The woman opposite him looked a little bemused. So Patterson pulled out his phone and used the translation function. He was able to show her *archaeological digs* in German. She gave a nod, picked up the phone and rang someone.

The woman then explained to Patterson that he needed to go to an office in a building half a mile away. She showed him where to go on a map of the island and Patterson smiled, thanked her, and left.

When he got to the office he'd been told to go to, he found a receptionist who then led him through the building to an almost hidey-hole of a place. It was more of a broom cupboard than an office, but one that contained a desk and a large number of books on shelves on the wall. Inside was an older man who smiled as if Patterson had been the only person to visit them so far in his lifetime.

'Do you speak English? I'm afraid my German's not very good,' said Patterson.

'Of course,' said the man. 'They said you were looking for information.'

'I was wondering, have there been any digs?'

'Digs? You mean archaeological digs? You mean looking for things from the past?'

'From back in the day of the Frisians,' said Patterson, knowing they were one of the earliest inhabitants of the islands.

CHAPTER 10

'There were a lot of digs in the north of Europe. I was just wondering if there were any items found.'

'I can't think of any registered digs,' the man said. 'Of course, a couple of hundred years ago, who knows, people used to loot places or just dig and not record fully.'

'But they would still be here, wouldn't they?' asked Patterson. 'You would see them on the surface.'

'Digs would have gone down or you would have dug into places with evidence. Certainly nothing on the surface at the moment. Anything that was down below—maybe they met something when they dug the tunnels—was not recorded.'

'I saw the tunnels,' said Patterson.

'All the tunnels are mapped. You didn't see them all.'

'But what about those that aren't on the visitor tour?'

'There are some. One that had a collapse back in the day. You realise that this place was bombed. They tried to blow it all up. A lot of the tunnels suffered damage. So now you have the tunnel that they've turned into a museum. The tunnels have no purpose today. Except as history to show what was.'

'But there are other tunnels?'

'Like I said, yes, but there's no access to it. It had a collapse. There are a few minor bits of tunnel that are used with the museum tunnel. They're connected to it, but they don't go any distance. Used mainly to store items for the museum tunnels.'

'That's a pity. I was hoping I might see something. Maybe I'll see something on the mainland.'

'I can recommend places to go on the mainland,' said the man.

'Oh, please do,' said Patterson.

He had another ten-minute conversation about sites on the mainland, just to keep his cover before he said goodbye to the man, thanking him for his time. Patterson left and he wandered around Heligoland, deciding to take a stroll. It was a good half an hour before he came to a cafe and sat down.

He could see Kirsten coming over, and she smiled and gave him a friendly wave. She sat opposite him on the table. They ordered two coffees, and she smiled, looking at him. 'Mother's fine,' she said, 'back at the apartment. Did you find out what you wanted? Any luck with your history tour?'

'Not so much. Got a lot of information about mainland sites.'

They waited until the coffees arrived, and Kirsten got in close. 'What's the real scoop?' she whispered.

'They said there's no other tunnels left. They all got bombed. Well, there's one, but it's got no access to it. There're just bits of tunnel that come off that main one we saw, the one used for the museum.'

'Well, I'm off,' said Kirsten. 'I need to do a hike. You go back to Mother,' she said loudly. 'I think she was getting grumpy.'

'Well, here she is.'

'Just couldn't wait. Well, I'm off before she rows with me,' said Kirsten. She disappeared as Clarissa arrived. She sat down with Patterson for a coffee, asking him nothing, instead just talking about the day.

After thirty minutes, she said she wanted to go back to the apartment. Patterson took her arm and helped her all the way back. Once they got inside the room, Clarissa shook her arm off him. 'Pretending I'm some sort of invalid. It's ridiculous,' said Clarissa.

'Didn't get much on my trip,' said Patterson. 'Problem is, a lot of the places were bombed here. So the tunnels that had been previously built, most of them caved in. They said there are a couple of small bits that are used by the museum, and

CHAPTER 10

there's one that's collapsed which doesn't have any access to it.'

'Well, there're no digs above ground,' said Clarissa. 'Your man didn't say that, did he?'

'No, he was saying there was no dig site.'

'Well, there's the potential for them to be underneath. They could be preserved. They could have found things at some point.'

'What does the information about the dig say? Does it describe it being above ground.'

'It doesn't say,' said Clarissa. 'It's talking about the site itself, so it being underground, that's always a possibility. There are no coordinates, just says Heligoland, top end of the island. So, up where that tunnel is, and around it, anywhere up there.'

'If it exists,' said Patterson.

'It'll exist. It may not be in the state it once was, but it'll exist,' said Clarissa. 'You don't write this sort of stuff, you don't kill people over this, if it doesn't exist. Something exists. And besides, Kirsten thinks you're being followed.'

'What?' blurted Patterson. 'I wasn't being followed.'

'Well, that's what the expert says. That's why she wanted time to go off. Find out what's going on.'

'But . . . what? Really?'

'Shocking, isn't it? We do our undercover work, and we think we know what we're about,' said Clarissa. 'But this stuff, it's on a different level. She's good, though. She's very good. I just wish she'd let me get on with it at times. She always wants to run the show. I can't see that worked out well in Italy with Macleod. I think she was over there with him. He doesn't talk about Italy much. Susan said they'd helped, but she's tight-lipped about it too.'

'What's our play, though?' said Patterson. 'We can't exactly turn up with a couple of diggers and start excavating the land up and around the tunnels. They might notice.'

'No,' said Clarissa, 'and a couple of spades at night won't do the job either. I think if there's a dig site, it's still there, somewhere. Whatever this is, is important, and it will still be there. But there must be access to it.'

The door sounded a special knock. Clarissa opened it to Kirsten, who stepped in looking worried.

'I tailed him. You were definitely tailed, Pats,' she said.

'You can call me Eric or Patterson, okay? My name isn't Pats.'

'Pats, don't be so ridiculous,' said Clarissa. 'Pats is fine.'

'You're being watched, Eric,' said Kirsten.

'So what's our next ploy? What do we do? How do we shake them? What's your ideas, Kirsten?' said Clarissa.

Kirsten gave a cough. 'We need to act like tourists for a bit. They were watching you, but they weren't suspecting you. They didn't go inside the building when you went to get your information. That means either they know the person in question inside, and he'll tell them what you said, or they're not that bothered. They're just keeping a very loose eye.

'Remember, they know something's up. So, they must know somebody is coming to Heligoland at some point. They don't know it's today. They don't know it's now. So, it may be just a loose watch on anybody different arriving. You may be one of many. You visited the tunnels. Does that mean the tunnels are important?'

'Possibly,' said Clarissa.

'The mention of dig sites. The mention of other things may be important. I don't know,' said Kirsten. 'Because we don't

CHAPTER 10

know what it is we're really looking for. It's a dig site, but we don't know what state it's in, do we?'

'Well, if you think about it,' said Clarissa, 'it's got to be something they're looking to protect. It's got to be something revered. Otherwise, what's the point of it? Take the goods out of it to hang on to and get rid of it. The knife came from somewhere. It came from here, possibly. That's what Dart seemed to indicate. But we don't know that for sure. Yet, if he's going on about it, there must be something here, there must be something to protect.'

'Let's go for a walk,' said Kirsten.

The threesome, arm in arm with Clarissa in the centre, walked up towards the museum. They then walked around, above ground, where the tunnels would have been. After an hour, Kirsten bought some ice creams, and they sat down on a bench, looking out to sea.

'We're still being watched,' said Kirsten. 'It's not a close tail, but they are watching what we're doing. Just eat your ice cream.'

'Can they hear us?' asked Clarissa.

'If I say yes, you've just blown our cover. I would have also blown our cover.'

'That's a good point,' said Clarissa. 'Sorry, not used to this.'

'No,' said Kirsten. 'But you're right with one thing. Why would you protect this? If there wasn't anything here, you wouldn't protect. So something's got to be here. So where is it? Is it a manuscript or some piece of paper?'

'Well, what sort of paper?' said Patterson. 'And if it's a bit of paper or something like that, why would you keep it here? Why wouldn't you just move it?'

'Could be tied to the place,' said Clarissa.

'But you're worried enough to kill,' said Patterson. 'You would just move it.'

'Unless it can't be moved,' said Clarissa. 'It might be something revered. We're talking about ritual. Dagger. We were talking about people who slit throats in a specific fashion. All from behind, all across the neck. Ritualistic killing. You don't kill ritualistically just for the laugh. You do it because you believe in it.'

'And when people believe in something,' said Patterson, 'there're often places that stir that belief, aren't there?'

'How do you mean?' asked Clarissa.

'Well,' said Patterson, 'Lourdes, healing waters. There's all the Catholic stuff where you see the Virgin Mary in different places. People in Ireland walk up St. Patrick's Hill. People have a place that they go to. UFO conspiracists, Area 51. Everybody's got something that they go to, a place, when they're that devoted to something. Even people devoted to nature will have places they go to. Druids used to gather in places.'

'Yes,' said Clarissa suddenly. 'Yes. Maybe there's a place. Maybe it's the place, not what they found. It's not the dig. It's the place. That's why they protect here. That's why they're on top of it.'

'I don't mean to be funny,' said Kirsten, 'but are we talking about something that's international? It's not just about cleaning up Scotland, is it? It's criminals.'

'I don't know,' said Clarissa, 'but this all smacks of a devotion, of a cult.'

'So, where do we look next?' said Kirsten.

'We look underneath. We look where they don't want us to look,' said Clarissa.

CHAPTER 10

'Patterson was told that the tunnel was blocked. Nowhere to go. No sites to look at. We need to check that out, make sure it's blocked. We need to make sure there's nothing underneath the ground here.'

'Well, we won't be doing that during the day,' said Kirsten. 'The museum's busy. We'd have to do it at night. Maybe I'd have to do it at night.'

'You can't go in on your own, Kirstie. That won't work.'

'I can handle myself,' said Kirsten. 'I have infiltrated places before. It's not a problem. I can get down there and tell you.'

'Tell us what?' said Clarissa. 'You wouldn't have a clue what you're looking at. You need to get me there.'

Kirsten looked over at Patterson, and he was nodding back.

'She's right,' he said. 'The one thing Macleod brought us in for, or rather more specifically, Clarissa, was the ability to understand and see what this dagger was. You could go in and you could miss something. You wouldn't know what you were looking at. Clarissa doesn't miss stuff around the arts, around artefacts, around things like that. She doesn't miss it. She's already talking about the type of thing we're looking for without having seen anything. This is her skill.'

'Thank you, Pats,' said Clarissa. 'I'm almost touched by that.'

'Whereas getting into places quietly and getting out again, disturbing nothing or causing any problems, is definitely not one of her skills. That's why you're here.'

'That's the best backhanded compliment I've ever had,' said Clarissa. 'Why are you here, then?'

'Probably to calm you down when you get overexcited.'

Kirsten nearly burst out laughing, but she held her face and looked at the pair of them.

'We go in and we'll have to go in tonight. They're watching

us. We will not stay that long, so we need to do something. I'll make a plan but when we go, you have to listen to me and you have to follow exactly. This won't be easy. On the other hand, it's a museum tunnel. It won't be that well protected. It'll be disguised. The best way to hide anything is to do it in plain sight, as part of something else.'

'Great,' said Clarissa. 'Okay, you get us in, quietly and unseen. I'll identify what's there, and Pats here will bring the fan and cold gel spray just to make sure I don't get overexcited.'

Patterson put his arm through Clarissa's and stood up, hauling her up to her feet. 'Come on, Mum. Time to get you back to the apartment.'

Chapter 11

It was two in the morning, and the small team of three were standing in the apartment. Clarissa looked over at Kirsten, dressed entirely in black. She cut the heck of a figure. The tight leggings, the top pulled tight around her, even the balaclava pulled down—she looked like something from a movie.

Clarissa looked at Patterson; he didn't look so menacing because he didn't have the physique, muscles to rival Kirsten's, but Patterson was trim. And yes, he looked more like a furtive beanpole than Kirsten's secret agent.

When she looked in the mirror, Clarissa nearly died off. The trouble with black leggings was that, for a woman of her age, it showed every curve. Every curve at her age was not the curves that you wanted to show. The top as well was designed for sleekness and mobility. But for Clarissa, she had clothing that held things in place, held her in place.

She wasn't designed for this Lycra thing. She wished she'd been consulted beforehand, but Kirsten had just asked for sizes. That was it. If ever she wanted her shawl around her, it was now. She wasn't fat. She wasn't overweight . . . actually, she was overweight. She knew she was overweight. But she wasn't that overweight. And she certainly wasn't overweight enough to look like this.

Kirsten looked at the three of them. 'Good,' she said. 'Remember, quiet voices everywhere we go. I'll tell you what to do. And when you do it, do it the way I've said. If I need you to do something, you'll be told. If you want to do something else, tell me first. We could be walking into places that are booby-trapped. So don't do it. Ask me first, or it may be the last action you take.'

'You're not serious,' said Clarissa. 'There's actually going to be places with what? Bombs?'

'Booby traps. Things that could kill you. We don't know what we're up against, but these people are lethal. You've seen the actions they take on people. They won't think twice about killing someone who's trying to invade their place. So, ask before you do.'

They disappeared from their apartment at two in the morning. Clarissa huffed and puffed as Kirsten took them on a circuitous route away from most of the buildings. Although it was early morning, it didn't mean that nobody was moving on Heligoland. The occasional person walked about, as they did anywhere. People that couldn't sleep, security patrols for businesses or local enforcement making sure that all was well at that time of the morning. They approached the museum, and Kirsten kept them low down in the grass.

'That's the main entrance there,' she said. 'From my scouting earlier on, there's an entrance round the back for the staff. We'll go in through there. It's just a locked door. It's not alarmed. Why would you alarm somewhere here? So out of the way. People couldn't get off the island anyway, if they were trying to steal something. Come on,' she said.

CHAPTER 11

Kirsten led them round the back of a few buildings, and into a door that Clarissa hadn't read. From inside her outfit, Kirsten produced some tools, and the door was opened inside of thirty seconds. She ushered them inside and then closed it behind her.

A small corridor had rooms off of it, and Clarissa's German was enough to see the word *Staff* on several of them. Changing areas. Maybe there was a canteen.

Kirsten led them out through another door that led into the entrance area. It was dark, but they could see the reception, where they had previously paid for their tickets when they had taken their tour of the tunnels. Kirsten stopped.

'What is it?' asked Clarissa.

Kirsten put her finger up to Clarissa's mouth. Clarissa watched Kirsten looking left and right. And then, cautiously, she pointed towards the main entrance doors. There was somebody on the outside checking them. You could see the door being pushed, but it was locked. And off they went, the footsteps disappearing from the door.

'Security checking, just making sure everything's locked.'

'You did lock that door behind us, didn't you?' said Clarissa. 'The one we came in.'

'I have done this before,' said Kirsten. 'With a lot less talking. Shush.'

Kirsten indicated the other two should remain while she scouted out into the hallway leading into the tunnel. She appeared back at a corner waving them on, and Clarissa tried to run along hunched, before she gave up and ran upright. Women of her age weren't designed for this. She couldn't run along while hunched over. Besides, Kirsten had to get her there. Clarissa was there for her expertise, her abilities, not for her athletic prowess.

It was different in the tunnel now than from their earlier visit. All the boards on the wall that had been backlit so you could read them had been switched off. There was an occasional emergency exit light, but otherwise, it was dark. However, the green glow from the emergency exit lights allowed them to see well. After walking up and down the main tunnels, Kirsten stopped them.

'Those are the main runs,' she said. 'We're going to explore the couple of turn-offs we haven't, the ones that say, *Staff Only*. It might be in there. We've covered everywhere else. I can't see anywhere with a fake door, or sliding access.'

'Are you for real?' said Clarissa. 'Sliding access, fake doors. You're telling me they're hiding a dig site down here?'

'How do you think it's going to be hidden?'

'In plain sight,' said Clarissa. 'That's what you said?'

'Exactly. Sliding doors are in plain sight. Come on.'

Kirsten led them over to a small alcove off one of the tunnels, chained off by a little plastic chain with a *Staff Only* sign on it. Kirsten took the chain off, and they passed through briefly before stopping.

'It's got a bit of a run here,' said Clarissa.

Kirsten put her hand up, indicating they should stay still. She disappeared down the tunnel briefly and then came back, waving them on. Clarissa walked down. In the green glow from the emergency exit light, she could see some storage on the right-hand side.

Clarissa's hands were gloved, and she pulled at some of the drawers in the storage unit. Pulling out the documentation, she saw lots of leaflets in different languages.

'This is just where they store their bumf,' said Patterson.

CHAPTER 11

'Look, this is the stuff you get when you're walking round. Adverts and different things. Nothing important in there.'

Clarissa nodded.

The team continued round a corner, where everything got a lot darker. There was no emergency exit light here. Kirsten turned round to Patterson. 'Eric. Go back round the corner. Listen and watch. You hear anything or you see anything, you come straight back to me.'

'What are we going to do?' asked Clarissa.

'We're going to explore in here.' Clarissa nodded and Patterson stepped back around the corner.

Kirsten took out a small pocket flashlight. The tunnel extended for at least another seven or eight metres. Kirsten handed the flashlight to Clarissa. 'Keep it trained on the wall all the way down. Say nothing. I'll show with my hands when I want you to move.'

Clarissa watched as Kirsten went up and down the wall, pushing at it, seeking for anything that wasn't one hundred per cent smooth. But the tunnel was smooth, neatly made, certainly not roughly hewn. This must have been part of the main tunnels, part of the extensive line that went somewhere in its day. So where would this go? It took them a painstaking ten minutes to move down the walls with Kirsten checking for traps until eventually Clarissa shone her light on a metal door.

'What do you make of that?' asked Kirsten.

'It's a pretty significant door, isn't it?'

'It is,' said Kirsten, pointing to the round handle. 'Like the wheel on a vault, or a submarine hatch, to lock it off. That's a door that says we don't go through there. This is locked off for a reason. It could be because the tunnel is unsafe beyond it. That's what Eric was told.'

'That could be the lie though, couldn't it?' said Clarissa. 'You said about being in plain sight. This could be the plain sight. Let's open it and find out.'

'Wait,' said Kirsten.

'Wait? We're out here in the dark. We're clearly where we shouldn't be. And you're telling me we should wait. The longer we wait, the more likely it is we get caught.'

'Remember, I said to you that these people will protect what they've got? Booby traps.'

'I don't see any booby traps there,' said Clarissa. 'It's just a door.'

'The point of booby traps is you don't see them,' said Kirsten. 'Take the flashlight round the door really slowly.' Kirsten took out her mobile phone.

'What are you doing?' said Clarissa.

'Taking photographs.'

'Why?'

'What do you mean, why? Because I need to get this checked out.'

'Can't you check it?' asked Clarissa.

'Look at it. Can you see anything?'

'No,' said Clarissa.

'Exactly. Flashlight. All the way round it, please. Slowly.'

Clarissa was feeling her feet getting tired. They'd been running around furtively and the whole tension of the night was getting to her. Her shoulders were sore, but she held the light up and watched as Kirsten's hands moved across the door.

'Look at this,' said Kirsten.

'Look at what?' said Clarissa, staring up at where the flashlight beam was.

CHAPTER 11

'There are wires running along underneath the wall here. You can feel the slight lift. And, connecting into the door, just here.'

She lifted her mobile up and took photos. She then went down to the hinges of the door, photographing them and all the way around.

'What are you thinking?' asked Clarissa.

'I'm thinking this door is wired. This door has got something on it, something that says when this door opens, something happens. Not sure what, though. I need somebody that knows about these things.'

'So what do we do? Are you going to phone someone?'

'I'm not sure I'm going to get a lot of signal down here. But I'll make contact back at the apartment.'

'So what, we're just going to go?' blurted Clarissa.

'Yes, we're going to go. Put everything back in the backpack. Let's get out of here.'

Before they could turn, Patterson appeared at the other end of the tunnel. His face was just about able to be made out, as he lifted his balaclava. He was mouthing the word *Someone*. Kirsten tore along the corridor, Clarissa following her, trying to stay as quiet as Kirsten moved.

'Where?' asked Kirsten in a hushed voice.

'Corridor, not far away.'

'Damn it,' said Kirsten, and pulled down Patterson's balaclava. She turned round the corner and then waved him through. They were back where all the leaflets were kept, and Kirsten looked on either side. There was a cupboard, tall enough for a person, and she opened it. Inside were several jackets and bibs. Kirsten grabbed Clarissa.

'In there, now,' she said. 'You too, Eric.'

The pair of them stepped inside, and Clarissa said, 'Where are you going?'

'Never you mind,' she said, and closed the door of the cupboard.

It was dark inside, but Clarissa could feel Patterson's breath expelling into the eye holes of her balaclava. She lifted the balaclava up, but Patterson pulled it back down. He couldn't see, but he could hear. He whispered ever so quietly, 'Best to stay covered up so they don't know who we are.'

She reached out, found his hand, squeezing it. They went silent completely, but they could hear movement in the tunnel. Steps came down. Someone was right outside the cupboard now. Were they looking around? They walked past the cupboard. Heavy boots, Clarissa thought. She could feel herself shaking. Where was Kirsten?

The boots came past again, slowly. Then, they moved away. Clarissa could feel herself quiver. It was dark. It was claustrophobic. She needed to get out. Needed to get away. The boots were gone, weren't they? They'd disappeared. She pushed at the door and it opened. Light flooded in. Despite being an emergency light, it was so bright compared to the utter darkness she'd just been in. She stepped out, Patterson following her.

'What the hell are you doing?' he said. 'Kirsten didn't tell us to come out.'

'Where is she?' said Clarissa.

She looked down the tunnel, but Kirsten wasn't there. She went round the corner into the other tunnel. It was pitch black. And then she heard a voice.

'You should be inside the cupboard,' it said very quietly and very slowly. Clarissa tilted her head back and looked up.

CHAPTER 11

Kirsten was up above her, her legs pushed out, along with her hands, supporting herself against the wall and up against the roof of the tunnel.

'Move a minute,' said Kirsten. Clarissa stepped back and Kirsten dropped to the floor as if it was the most natural thing in the world. 'We'll talk about this later,' said Kirsten, stepping past Clarissa. 'Follow me.'

Kirsten quickly took them back the way they'd come. She would stop occasionally, listening. But as she got to the door that they'd entered from, Kirsten swore. There were footprints. A little dust.

'They won't notice that, will they?' said Clarissa.

Kirsten nodded. It wasn't much, but it was enough. 'Our presence will have been noted,' she said, undoing the lock on the door. She snuck them out, closed the door, locked it, and then took them back round another circuitous route. Inside her balaclava, Clarissa was sweating heavily. She kept going, wanting desperately to get back into the apartment. It felt like the only safe place now. Would people be out looking for them?

Kirsten held them up before going into the apartment. She went in and checked it, and surveyed all around.

By half four in the morning, Clarissa was in the apartment. Entering the room, Clarissa whipped off her balaclava and threw it on the bed.

Kirsten took her own off, shaking out her long black hair, and then turned to the other two, putting her finger up to her mouth.

'We stay quiet. Remember, we'd be asleep. No lights,' she said. They took turns with the bathroom to get changed. Soon, under Kirsten's instruction, they were all lying in bed. Kirsten had told them to get some sleep.

But Clarissa was lying, almost shaking. She thought of Frank. He'd be worried about her. Anxious. This was a unique feeling Clarissa was experiencing. Normally, when there was art, she charged in. She didn't look back, but right now she was terrified. It was taking everything she'd got to stay calm. If there was a dig site here, it would be so ancient, and probably so worth seeing. Yet part of her would take the option of jumping on a ferry and getting out of here the next day.

Chapter 12

Macleod parked his car up outside Clarissa's house and stepped out into a cold and breezy morning. It was that time of year in Inverness. You got some good days; you got some rough days. But the weather was on the change. In truth, Macleod was nervous. He didn't like it that Kirsten had gone dark, but he understood. She had to cut off communications, and had to make sure he didn't get fed anything because she needed to be completely aloof. Completely undetectable. She was out of the country. She didn't have her normal stash of places to run to, the old Service haunts she could use in an emergency.

Kirsten also had two people with her who were not used to being out there. Macleod thought Patterson would cope well with it. He was good at seeing situations and adapting to them. He adapted to Clarissa, after all. But Clarissa wasn't like that. Clarissa was a force of nature. He also thought she would be scared, because she wouldn't be in control.

Macleod remembered Italy. He remembered Kirsten coming out there and how he thought he was in charge. He thought he was clever, but the level that Kirsten worked at was different. There wasn't a decency there. There wasn't a fear like some criminals had. Yes, he was a detective, and a criminal would put him on his backside, but you didn't just kill people indiscriminately. That wasn't something you did. There were consequences when you got caught. But in Kirsten's game, the consequences were instant death. So you took people out and made sure they didn't get back up.

He didn't like that.

One other thing Macleod really didn't like was bringing in people on the outside. Frank was one of these people. He was attached to Clarissa, and therefore, he could be a potential target. He was also helping run the scam that Clarissa was laid up after an operation.

Macleod could see Perry's car there as well. The others in his team had been good. Really good. They hadn't hounded him to find out about Clarissa and what she was doing. They'd taken on their role, and Perry's was to keep an eye on Frank. Perry wasn't quite a similar age to Clarissa. She was closer to Macleod's age. But Perry seemed to be that touch older than the rest, possibly someone Frank would get on with. As Macleod approached the door, he saw Perry in the hallway. He opened the door to Macleod.

'How's things?' asked Macleod, stepping in. 'Is our patient well?' he said, trying not to say it too loudly. This was an act after all, not pantomime.

'Our patient's getting on with it. Grumpy as ever,' said Perry, before shutting the door. Once it was shut and he had turned around, Perry said, 'Frank's okay. He's in the living room at the moment. We're just watching a bit of sports.'

'What sport's on?' asked Macleod.

'Oh, it's golf.'

'Of course, it's golf. Frank likes golf. He's not getting fed up,

CHAPTER 12

is he?'

'He's worried,' said Perry. 'Of course, he's worried about her. And having two weeks off and kicking about the house because he's looking after *the patient* hasn't helped that.'

'Seen anyone about the house?'

'Well,' said Perry. 'Not particularly. There has been a new person, I think, driving past.'

'Really?' asked Macleod. 'Where?'

'Come upstairs.' Perry stuck his head in the door to the living room. 'We're just going upstairs a minute, Frank, okay? I just want to show the inspector something.'

They trailed upstairs to where Clarissa was meant to be recuperating. Once up there, Perry went over to the blinds of the bedroom, lifted them slightly, and looked out. Macleod stood beside him.

'It's coming past every sort of, oh, fifteen, twenty minutes,' he said. 'Should be due soon. Previously driven past in a car, though she might walk past this time.'

It took a moment, but then a woman in a black jacket walked past. She had long, red hair and was maybe in her forties.

'I have to say, if I was putting somebody on to watch this house, I wouldn't be so obvious.'

'I think she's meant to be obvious,' said Macleod.

'In what way?' asked Perry.

'Well, at the moment, because of what's going on, I'm going to be on edge. That red-headed woman—she's from Anna Hunt. Is Anna Hunt protecting us? Or is she watching us? Those up above who have talked to Anna Hunt will think she's just doing a job. And if the lady reports Clarissa is up here, even better.'

'You're getting good at this spy game, aren't you?' said Perry.

'No,' said Macleod. 'I hate it. I hate all this running around in the dark. It's not proper policing.'

'So what do I do with the red-haired woman? Just let her go?'

'Just let her be. I've seen her around me as well. She's been around the rest of the group. Anna Hunt will try to put some sort of protection around us. Anna's on our side. Well, she's on the good side. We've got nothing to fear from that woman. She may even be useful if things go south.'

'South?' queried Perry.

'Yes,' said Macleod. 'Don't ask me how and don't ask me where and when. But yes, south.'

They returned down to the living room, where Macleod shook Frank's hand. The man was clearly worn out by everything.

'How is she?' asked Frank.

'Last I saw her, she was fine,' said Macleod. 'However, it's been a while since I've had contact. That's all I'm saying. However, she gave me this for you.' Macleod handed over the letter that Clarissa had written in the Brighton hotel room. Macleod watched as he read it. The man didn't seem to be reassured, but rather, more worried.

'You okay?' asked Macleod.

'What have you got her doing?' asked Frank and then he put his hand up. 'You can't tell me. I get it; shouldn't know. I get it. She's worried. Maybe petrified. How important is this that she's doing it?'

'They killed one of our own,' said Macleod.

Frank nodded. 'And she'll get them,' he said. 'You want to get them too, don't you?'

'What we're doing is . . . well . . . ,' said Macleod. 'I can't tell

CHAPTER 12

you, but it's important. It's very important. More important than police work.'

'Well,' said Perry. 'The inspector likes a coffee. Should I get them, Frank?'

'No, no, I'll get it. Give me something to do.' Frank turned to walk out of the room, but then he turned back to the TV. 'How do you miss that? Tell me. See that, Perry? How do you miss that putt?' And then Frank was out to the kitchen.

'Do you think she told him?' asked Macleod.

'No,' said Perry. 'She's written him a letter to say that she's okay, and he's not to worry and she's fine and that. And he's anxious now because she doesn't write letters like that.'

'No, she doesn't,' said Macleod. 'She tears off and leaves him behind at the nearest art thing. And now she's writing him a note. She thinks she might not come back.'

'I wouldn't put it like that if Frank comes in here again.'

'Of course not,' said Macleod.

'Is she all right?' asked Perry.

Macleod raised his shoulders. *How would I know?*

'I heard about your secretary,' said Perry. 'Not really what you need either, is it?'

'It's not what she needs,' said Macleod. 'I'm going to see her after this. At least she's out of the way from all this. It's going to be tough, though. Not someone there I can trust at the moment. It's not like I can get Susan to come in and cover.'

'Can't you just get an office worker or something?'

'I can't,' said Macleod. 'Could be a plant. And I don't know anyone who could come in and do it. Don't want to lift anybody up from the ranks into this. Need to keep it tight. Need to keep it with people who have got a head for it. Can't think of anyone,' said Macleod. He sat down on the sofa, and

Perry thought he was not himself.

'You kind of relied on her, didn't you?'

'I've always relied on people to pick up that side. Sorting my admin. But even more so now. It has to be tight. They have to spot other things coming. A person who needs to be well aware of everything.'

'Can you take a bit of advice?' asked Perry.

'You're dishing out advice now? Not like you.'

'Well no,' said Perry. 'Can I give you a suggestion? Of a person?'

'Who?'

'Tanya,' said Perry. 'She works HR down in Glasgow.'

'Glasgow? Seriously? You want to bring somebody up from the Glasgow side at the moment? Glasgow is where we had half the problem. I think there's a nest of vipers in there,' said Macleod.

'Tanya won't be one of them, and if there is a nest of vipers down there, Tanya will want to see them put away.'

'How do you know her?'

'She worked in HR. That's probably why you don't know her that well. You never enjoyed talking to HR, did you?'

'I wasn't aware you did,' said Macleod.

'I didn't,' said Perry, 'but I liked talking to Tanya. We were, well, we weren't intimate, but we were close for a while, and then, well, I kind of threw a spanner in the works.'

'How?' asked Macleod.

'She went to get married,' said Perry. 'She was going to marry this guy, he was a . . . oh, he was an arsehole. Sorry, you don't like that sort of language.'

'It's coming from you, I'm sure it's accurate,' said Macleod. 'Go on.'

CHAPTER 12

'Well, I told her that. I told her in no uncertain terms and we kind of spoke little after that. When I went down to Glasgow, she was the only one who would speak to me. She was the one who got me the information to find out about Barrington's disability. Without a request. Without a formal request because I asked for it or because we were looking into stuff. Tanya's a good person. She's also that bit older. She'll understand what to look for. And if you need her to do something outwith . . . she's got a head on her to do it. She's a clever cookie. Tanya's also open to getting away from down there. Got some memories to put behind her.'

'And you'd be happy to see her up here?' asked Macleod.

'Tanya's a good person.'

'Anything happened between the two of you when you were down there?'

'It's not like you to ask that,' said Perry.

'I haven't been in these times often.'

'If you must know, yes. She'd be happy to see me again, but we're not on that level . . . It's just we thought that you and—'

'Me and who?'

'Susan. Well, Hope seemed to think—'

'Hope seemed to think what? You can tell me,' said Macleod. 'It's difficult starting again. I couldn't do it for a long time,' said Macleod, 'not until I found Jane.'

'Look, between you and me,' said Perry. 'Susan, yes, I like Susan despite her being a bit younger. But Susan wasn't interested, and she's a friend now, and we're good colleagues and that. But I don't know; I don't know. Tanya, well, you see, Tanya, me and her are the same age. Got a lot of things in common. Maybe it would work; maybe it wouldn't. Nice to have her around, though. Even just on a friend basis.'

Macleod had never known Perry to waffle so much. He must have had deep feelings for the woman. 'You trust her?'

'With my life. And she's shrewd. She can handle grumpy people. So, you'll be no problem. And she's very trustworthy.'

'You got a direct number?' asked Macleod.

'Yes,' said Perry. He passed Tanya's mobile number to Macleod. Macleod stood up, put his head around the door to shout to Frank. 'Mind if I use your phone?'

'Sure,' said Frank.

'Are you sure there's not a tap on the phone?' asked Perry.

'There's nothing on this line,' said Macleod, 'and if there is, it'll be Anna Hunt. I'm sure there's nothing on this line and if I don't use my mobile, then they can't trace that I've been talking to Tanya. In the first instance, I can get her a secondment, then we'll do it properly. I also need someone sharp, so interviews and the full job can be put off for a while.'

Frank emerged with some coffees and handed one to Macleod. He took his outside to the hallway and picked up the phone. Perry resumed watching the golf with Frank but he could tell Frank was agitated by the letter.

Macleod came back in, looking satisfied with himself.

'Any news?' asked Perry.

'Tanya's coming up. She'll be up here tomorrow. You can give her a hand with places to stay and that. I'm looking forward to meeting her,' said Macleod. 'She had a few tough questions for me. Proper questions.'

Perry smiled. 'She'll be good for you,' he said. 'Really good.'

'I hope so,' said Macleod. 'I really do.' He sat back and the three men watched the television for the next five minutes. There was silence, each in their own thoughts. Then Macleod suddenly said, 'Frank, how on earth do people play this game?

CHAPTER 12

How do you not get bored hitting that wee ball?'

'You are so lucky,' said Frank suddenly. 'So lucky Clarissa's not here. She'd have thrown you out of the house for that comment.'

The three of them smiled for a moment. And then Perry said, 'I'd have liked to have seen that.

'That was out loud, Perry,' said Macleod. 'Watch it.'

Chapter 13

Clarissa woke up the next morning to see Kirsten sitting at the small table within their apartment, messaging on her phone. Clarissa ignored her, went to the shower, washed, came back and changed, before sitting down with a coffee and a croissant.

'You're a long time on that,' she said.

'He needed to contact some old friends. A man called Justin. He knows about this sort of thing, or at least knows people who do. Had to send some photos.'

'And so what do we do while you're doing all this?' said Clarissa.

'I believe . . . we're going out for the day. I asked Eric to make us some plans. Places to visit, go out for lunch, something like that.'

'Why?'

'Until I get back what I need to know, we are not going back to that place. We're not going to the museum. We've been once already, so we shouldn't be going back if we're a tourist family. Why would you go back in? We'll go down to the beach; we'll walk around the coast. Let's do anything else, visit places. Chill out, we'll just be a family. Okay? Mum with her

CHAPTER 13

two kids.'

'Really?' said Clarissa. 'You know I'm exhausted. We were up half the night.'

'And you could be up half the night tonight as well, and more than that. We could be up half the night and getting out of here,' said Kirsten. 'We'll not do anything too strenuous. We'll sit, we'll eat, we'll relax but we need to be out and doing. You don't put your feet up in an old apartment simply because you're on holiday. The weather's good; we should be outside enjoying it. You need to keep the cover up at all times.'

'Okay,' said Clarissa.

Kirsten stopped typing on her phone and looked over at Clarissa. 'You okay?' she said.

'I'm just tired.'

'You're living on your nerves,' said Kirsten. 'You need to stop living on your nerves. This thing we do, it's just what we do. It's like being a police officer. When you arrest someone or whatever, it's the first day—it's a big deal. When you do it after that, you just do it. Everything you do, you just do because it's police work. If everything was a big deal every day, you'd be emotionally shattered. This is just what we do.'

'This is just what you do,' said Clarissa. 'Me? Pats? It's not what we do. Pats will be exhausted too. Pats' nerves will be shattered. This is scaring the living daylights out of me, and I was the one who knelt and held his throat together when he was dying. And this scares me much more.'

'Because you've got somebody waiting for you. That's what scares you. You wrote that letter to Frank,' said Kirsten.

'I didn't tell him anything.'

'No, but you wrote it. You normally write him letters? Normally say anything to him when you charge about? From the way Macleod described you to me, you were not exactly gung-ho, but super-focused when the arts world came. You didn't hold back for anybody else. Not even Frank.'

Clarissa went slightly red in the face. 'No, I don't, and I have never written him a letter before.'

'I would've suggested that you didn't, but it's up to you. He'll probably be more worried now. But don't worry, I'll get you back.'

'You say that with confidence,' said Clarissa. 'You don't really know, though, do you?'

'We don't really know much about anything,' said Kirsten. 'But I believe it. Believe it. Everything you do in this job, in this line of work, you must believe it. And the things you don't believe, the things you don't know, examine them. I know I'll get out. I know I'll get you out.'

'Glad somebody's confident,' said Clarissa.

The rest of the day was spent having lunch and dinner and moseying about on Heligoland. There wasn't a lot to see, or at least nothing that was interesting, for Clarissa's mind was too focused on the job. Several times Kirsten told her to look more attentive to what they were doing, but it was an act, and one Clarissa had to force.

That evening, Clarissa challenged Kirsten about going out that night.

'No,' said Kirsten. 'We won't go tonight. I need some equipment. And they've messaged back about that door. I am not going through that door without the equipment I need. It's too risky.'

'So what do we do?'

'You go to bed. Pats and you get to bed. I will go to bed shortly. We sleep, recover, recuperate. Tomorrow we might have to pretend to be tourists again. If you have to take some drinks, drink something and get to sleep. But if you can manage without, all the better because your body will recover better for it.'

'And that's it? That's your advice?'

'That's all there is,' said Kirsten. 'I'm running this, and that's what we're doing. So, get on with it.'

Clarissa nodded reluctantly and disappeared off to her bed. The next morning, the three of them took another tour of the island. There was more coffee. Clarissa didn't think she could get bored with sitting and drinking coffee in what was a beautiful place. But she did, and she was struggling to hide it.

'I have to go out this afternoon,' said Kirsten. 'Mother's going to be too tired. I want you to go back to the apartment and get some sleep. We go tonight.'

'Thank goodness for that,' said Clarissa.

That afternoon, Kirsten made her way down to where the fishermen hung out around the port. It wasn't a large port, big enough to take the ferries in and for the many fishermen that were there. But Kirsten was looking for someone, specifically Jürgen Kant.

A package had been delivered to him that he wasn't sure about it. And besides, it didn't say Jürgen Kant on it. It said Jorgen. J-O-R-G-E-N.

But the address was the port on Heligoland. A general address. And someone had decided that it must be for Jürgen. After all, the spelling was wrong. The address was dodgy. Maybe they just didn't know. Jürgen, however, wasn't expecting a package. But Kirsten was.

She arrived at the port and asked if there was a list of people. She said she was looking for someone, a person at the port.

The port authority asked who, but she said it was an old friend and never actually clarified who. Looking down the list, she spotted Jürgen Kant's name and his boat. Kirsten knew the boat would be there, for Justin had organised this misdelivery of a package. She walked along and spotted the man on the quayside, the only one on his fishing boat. She approached. 'Would you be Jürgen Kant?' she asked in German.

He nodded.

'You might have something of mine. I got a notification a package had been delivered, but it hadn't, and it occurred to me that there might be somebody with a similar name here on Heligoland.'

'Okay,' said Jürgen. 'You are?'

Kirsten stepped forward to the edge of his boat and pulled out a passport. It said 'Jorgen Kant' on it. It had taken her maybe a half an hour to work on it, and it wasn't a forgery that would stand up to any rigorous examination. Just a passport she would use on the fly if she had to, to flash in front of people who didn't really know about documentation. She had put the name in herself. Jorgen.

'Jorgen's a funny name.'

'Yes, it is,' said Kirsten. 'Named after my grandfather. Spelt wrong, though, when they registered the birth.'

'But Jorgen's a boy's name.'

'Wasn't a German family I came from. Misunderstanding, but I keep it. Because it's Jorgen, not Jürgen.'

The man looked at the false ID, gave a nod, and handed the package over. Kirsten returned to the apartment.

As she put it down on the table, Clarissa emerged from her bedroom, wrapped up in the dressing gown that came with the apartment. 'What's in there then?' she asked.

CHAPTER 13

Kirsten opened it up. 'Well,' she said, 'I've got some cutting gear. That'll get us through the door. I've got some electrical gadgetry. That should hopefully neutralise the wiring that's attached to the door. And I've got some powder.'

'What's the powder for?'

'The powder goes over all of this. When I go, there won't be anything left of this. The powder will have taken care of it. Have you packed?' asked Kirsten.

'Yes I have,' said Clarissa. 'We're ready to go when you are.'

'Back to bed then,' said Kirsten. 'Be ready at one.'

At one o'clock in the morning, the three were gathered in the apartment, dressed in their black outfits again. The rest of their clothing was now in the small bags they brought with them. Kirsten disappeared with the bags for twenty minutes before coming back without them.

'They're secure. We'll get them on the way when we leave. There's nothing else left in the apartment,' she said, 'because we aren't coming back? Let's get going.'

Clarissa and Patterson nodded and together they made their way back towards the tunnels. As they got close, Kirsten told Clarissa and Patterson to get down.

'You stay here.'

'What's wrong?' asked Clarissa.

'There's somebody else here. Not the security guard. He was anybody, an old Joe Bloggs. There's somebody else watching the place.'

'You can see them?' asked Clarissa. 'I can't see anyone.'

Kirsten pointed. 'Watch there,' she said, 'carefully.'

Clarissa looked. She couldn't see anything. There were a couple of trees and grassland, up towards the rear of the building that provided the reception for the museum tunnels.

'Keep watching,' said Kirsten slowly.

Clarissa kept watching. And then, ever so suddenly, something moved. There was a quick change of colour. The blacks of the night suddenly were dark greens, or was it a very dark blue? Shades that moved.

'Something there,' she said. 'Could have just been shadows, though. Something being blown.'

'Could have been, couldn't it?' said Kirsten. 'But those were no shadows. I'll be back.'

She disappeared off, and Clarissa looked at Patterson. He just gave a nod. Clarissa could tell he was shaking inside as much as she was.

Kirsten came back about ten minutes later.

'Where is he?' asked Clarissa.

'He's not waking up. Certainly not until tomorrow afternoon.'

'Where'd you put him?'

'He's in a nearby building. They might find him before that, but not until the morning and we'll be gone. Besides, he never saw who did it to him.'

'They still don't know it's us?' said Clarissa.

'No, and let's hope they don't.'

Kirsten pulled her balaclava back down and told the other two to follow her. They crept up on the building again, going in through the same route they'd used the previous time. Slowly, they made their way through the tunnels, but there was no sign of anyone there. The other guard was on the outside.

Maybe that was the plan. The trouble with watching something too much was if there were normal security people around, they might spot you. Especially if you went inside. And that just made things awkward. So, it was better to watch

CHAPTER 13

the building from the outside to see if anyone was going in. The interior should be clear.

They arrived back at the tunnel that was for *Staff Only*, past the drawers and the cupboard where they'd hidden.

'Right,' said Kirsten. 'This is where it gets tricky. You need to listen and do. Okay? Watch behind me, Patterson. Anybody comes, let me know.'

She took out her cutting device and ignited it. Clarissa couldn't see where the gas canister was for it but clearly there was something and it burnt incredibly hot. It was like some sort of mini welding torch.

'Do you not need the electrical stuff?'

'Hopefully not,' said Kirsten. 'Not if this goes right. We think it's booby trapped, but if I can get the door open without actually opening it, I should be able to spot it and disable it from the other side. At least that's what they tell me.'

'You mean they don't know for sure?' asked Clarissa.

'How can we know for sure? Stuff's on the other side,' said Kirsten.

'So what? This could just set off the booby trap.'

'Confidence,' said Kirsten. 'It could, and we'll deal with it. Confidence.'

Kirsten took the cutting device, and Clarissa watched as the bright light in front of her cut through the metal door. Kirsten was shielding her eyes as she did so, and it was truly bright. But the residue behind showed red on the metal, and slowly the door was being cut through.

Kirsten went all the way up to the top of the door, and round and down, cutting a door out within the door. As she got down to the bottom, she used the wheel handle to pull the door towards her. She hadn't cut through the very bottom, and so, like a large flap, it came towards them, gently setting down onto the floor.

'Well, that's good,' she said. She looked up at the interior. 'The wiring's still intact. No booby trap on that one,' she said. 'But this, I don't like.'

Clarissa shone the torch, and there was a rock face beyond the door. 'So it's just been blocked up,' said Clarissa.

'Just been blocked, like they said in the office,' agreed Pats.

'Maybe.' Kirsten's hands began to feel around on the rock face. And then, much to Clarissa's surprise, the rock face was pushed back, opening out to another tunnel.

'What's that?' asked Clarissa.

'That's your false door. You don't just put a door in and say what's behind it. When you open it, you see what's behind it. And that's why nobody bats an eyelid about this door. They know it's rock behind it, except it isn't. There's this tunnel.'

It was dark in the tunnel beyond. Completely dark. Clarissa took her torch. Patterson looked back to see how they were getting on, and Kirsten told him to follow her. Stepping inside the tunnel beyond the false rock face, Kirsten suddenly stopped.

A flashing device was on the wall. It hadn't been there a moment ago. At least it hadn't been flashing. It had just been darkness. Clarissa automatically shone her light over towards it.

'Oh, shit!' said Kirsten.

'What?' blurted Clarissa.

'Second device,' said Kirsten. 'Booby trap!'

Chapter 14

'What do you mean, booby trap?' said Clarissa.

Kirsten pointed to the wall. 'That, the bloody flashing thing.' Kirsten ran over and stared at the device. It was rectangular, flush on the wall, and had a keypad.

'What's that?' asked Clarissa.

'This is what they press to switch it off. Well, I haven't got something that can override that.' Kirsten pulled at the front cover. She yanked it hard, and it came away. 'No, no, this is just a keypad. It's not the central device. Damn it,' she said. Kirsten dropped her backpack, turned and started digging in it. 'Look for it. Look for another one. There's going to be another electrical device in here.'

'What's it look like?' asked Clarissa.

'It'll have wires. It'll have a front on it. Plastic. Whatever.'

Clarissa started looking around desperately and Patterson joined as well. Clarissa held the main torch and began moving along the tunnel. However, it wasn't a smooth tunnel wall like previously. This had been carved out and then not patched up to make a modern tunnel. It made her think. *This isn't part of the tunnels that were built here. This hasn't been blocked off. Well, it's been blocked off deliberately. We must be—*

'Look!' said Clarissa, suddenly seeing the other electrical device.

Kirsten burst in forcefully. 'We've only got a minute or two. All it will do is give a stay of execution so they can get out of here in case they've messed up with the numbers.'

Clarissa looked around frantically. She could hear something.

'Pats,' she said. 'Do you hear stuff? Do you hear footsteps?' Patterson nodded.

'Kirstie, there's somebody outside. You'll need to go to them.'

'I need to deal with this bomb,' said Kirsten, pulling out an electrical gizmo. 'If I don't, whoever's out there is irrelevant. We'll all be blown to kingdom come.'

Clarissa looked at her, wondering what to do. *Oh well*, she thought, *if she can't solve it, I'll have to deal with it. Besides, what good am I with a bomb?*

Clarissa put the torch down beside Kirsten and turned for the gap that led back out to the initial tunnel. As she got through and out to the first door they'd cut down, Clarissa could hear the footsteps more clearly. She stepped out onto the metal door that now lay on the floor and, as she did so, a man turned at the end of the corridor.

He said something and Clarissa believed it was a swear in whatever language he spoke, probably German. The man was turning to run, but Clarissa looked to her left and amongst the filing cabinets and drawers where the paperwork was, she saw a pointing stick.

It wasn't that long, but it would suffice. She reached over, grabbed it, and flung it along the tunnel. It tripped the man's heels as he turned to go, doing enough to cause him to stumble and then fall to the ground. She tore off up the corridor after him.

He was down and prone on the floor. Now was her opportunity.

She leapt forward, landing with her knees driving into his back, causing the man to exhale sharply. Clarissa grabbed his head, putting an arm around his throat, and she began pulling tightly. She wasn't quite sure what she was going to do with him. When would she stop? She didn't know. She just knew she had to hold him.

The man wasn't choking that well. In truth, Clarissa wasn't sure she had the strength to throttle him properly. Maybe she should take the arm off and use her hands. For now, her arm was wrapped around him, such that the front of his throat was where her elbow was. She wasn't sure it was constricting his airflow enough.

Clarissa watched as the man put one hand out in front of him, then another. And then slowly, despite her attentions, he lifted to try to stand with Clarissa still on his back. She kneed at his back but was also desperately hanging on with her arms.

The man got up. It was slow, but he got onto both feet. Clarissa clung to him, but the man simply drove backwards, slamming her up against the wall. For a moment, she felt like she was going to slip. But he was leaning back, holding her against the wall. Otherwise, she was sure she would have dropped. He'd move away soon, though.

Again, she pulled tight, hauling herself to him. She didn't fight like this. She wasn't someone who could trade punches. So Clarissa leaned forward and bit hard into the man's ear. He howled, but then he raised his fist and drove it right beside his head and behind. It caught her and her arms went loose.

He stepped forward, and she fell off his back and onto the

floor. The man was quicker than her, and besides, the punch had stunned Clarissa. He reached down, and she could see his strength as he lifted her up and pinned her against the wall. His hands flew to her throat, throttling her.

Her legs were kicking now, trying to find any sort of purchase, but the man was at a distance almost the length of his arms. She tried to swing them out and succeeded in kicking him in the side. But then he stepped closer, his elbows bending. He said something in German. Clarissa's German wasn't bad, but right at this moment, her brain wasn't focusing too well.

Clarissa wanted to cry for help. Kirsten was meant to be here. Kirsten was meant to protect her against people like this. It wasn't the first time that Clarissa had been throttled, but this time, the thumbs were pushing in. She almost felt like the man could snap her neck. And she was helpless, legs kicking aimlessly now, arms down by her side.

And then she thought of it. She carried the ritual knife on her, not wanting to leave it anywhere. It was inside her jacket. She reached to her jacket, unzipped the pocket on her right-hand side, and reached in. The knife was there in a plastic cover, but she grabbed it.

Before she removed it, however, she forced herself to rummage around her mouth with her tongue, finding every bit of spittle she could. She spat into the man's face. She saw him get angrier, react, push towards her, and then she took the knife and drove it into his side. The hands fell off her throat, and he stumbled backwards.

She drove the knife in twice more, as she fell down onto her feet, surprising herself as she could stand. She sucked in the first breath in a while and watched as the man fell down to the ground. Clarissa stepped forward and kicked him hard in the head. She then fell to her knees, gasping for air.

* * *

'Rummage along the wall, Patterson. Anything you can find, Eric. Just anywhere. It's got to be there somewhere. It might be hidden underneath. They can disguise them. They run the wires under the walls. Looks like a natural wall, but they'll run the wire in so you can't see it.'

Patterson wasn't quite sure what she meant, but his torch was scanning now, back and forward along the wall. Outside, he could hear a commotion but he had to focus. He had to do it.

'Come on,' said Kirsten. She spun round and started going down the other side of the wall. But Patterson suddenly felt something give way in his hand. He was up above the keypad and across to the right. Some part of the wall came loose in his hand, almost like dust.

He looked up and hit it, punching at the area. His hands were sore, but he forced himself to hit as hard as he could. 'This is coming away,' he said. 'It's coming away.'

Kirsten jumped over, shone her torch on it, and then turned and dived into her bag. She came out with what looked like a small pick and handed it to Patterson.

'Clear it, clear it all the way around the wire. Let's see where it's going.'

She was up with another box of tricks though, scanning the wall. Patterson went at the wall with fervour, and soon, he could see a black wire underneath. He reached in and started to pull at it. It was fairly loose, not the neatest of jobs, but then again, how much time would they have had to set all this up?

'Pull at it,' said Kirsten, joining Patterson. They pulled hard, and slowly some plaster work on the wall came away. It was cleverly disguised though, looking just like rock, except it wasn't. It was plaster that had been painted on, plaster that had been formed with jagged edges here and there. They pulled hard, until suddenly, it wouldn't come away from the wall. It had run two metres down. Kirsten now shone the torch. 'It's turning,' she said to Patterson. 'It's turning.'

Patterson took the pick and started working below the wire. Soon more wall was coming away and he could quickly see the wire descending.

'Pull again,' said Kirsten. They pulled down, and then it stopped.

'Why is it not coming away anymore?'

'Give me the pickaxe,' said Kirsten. She took it and slammed it into the area below where the wire had stopped coming out. Dust flew here and there, and Patterson held the torch on it so Kirsten could keep going.

'That's it,' she said. 'That's it, take this and keep going,' she said to him, handing him the pick.

Patterson held his torch with one hand and operated the pick with the other. He chipped away, revealing a plastic box. It was screwed down on either side.

'Do you have a screwdriver?' he said.

'Just break the damn box open!'

Patterson dug in, and the pick went into the plastic, but held there. Putting the torch down, he reached in and rolled the pickaxe round, levering it against the box. He heard a crack. He put the torch back up, saw he'd broken a line in the box, but the pickaxe was still stuck in. Patterson pulled and yanked again until he heard more cracking and had to re-look with the torch. There was a gap into it now.

'Hold the torch on it for me,' said Kirsten. She was attaching something electrical inside the box and looking at a readout.

Patterson watched in awe as she punched in something on the keypad of her device. He could smell her anxiety. Although it was cold and dank, the moment caused them both to sweat. They still had balaclavas on after all. She seemed to work quickly and then, all of a sudden, she stopped.

'What's up?' he said.

'Done. It's disabled.'

Patterson sat down on the floor but Kirsten was up again.

'Clarissa needs help,' she said.

She marched off out of the tunnel and through to where Clarissa would be, Patterson following. As she stepped out back into the main tunnel, in the green glow of the emergency exit light, Kirsten gasped. A man lay on the floor, blood running from his side. He looked unconscious. Was he dead?

'What have you done?'

'You were meant to protect me,' said Clarissa. She was sitting on the floor, propping herself up against the wall. Beside her, the knife was in its plastic bag, except it had punched through it with the blade, and the blade was covered in blood.

'He throttled me. He throttled me up against the—'

'I'll never make a secret agent of you,' said Kirsten. But she went over to the man, and knelt down beside him.

'Is he dead?' asked Clarissa.

'Not yet,' said Kirsten. 'Did he lift your balaclava at all?'

Clarissa shook her head. It was up now though, so Clarissa could breathe.

'Put it back down,' said Kirsten. 'We need to get on the move.'

Patterson had walked over to Clarissa and was kneeling down beside her. 'You okay?' he said. She shook her head.

'He gave me no choice, Pats. I didn't have a choice. He was strangling me, he was . . .'

'Yes, it's not the same rules out here,' said Patterson, 'but we need to get up and get going.'

'Did you get the bomb?'

'Yes, we've stopped it,' said Patterson.

'Then we're okay,' said Clarissa.

'We are not okay. We've got a half-dead man here,' said Kirsten. 'There's blood everywhere. We've ripped the door down. We're done. We're gone.'

'Can't be gone yet,' said Clarissa. 'Pats, tell her we can't be gone yet.'

'If she says we need to go. We'll need to go. She's here to look after us,' said Patterson.

'Fat lot of use that was,' said Clarissa.

'Gather the stuff, Patterson,' said Kirsten.

'Pats, don't you dare,' said Clarissa. 'We've come this far. I've just stabbed a guy. I didn't come here to not know what's in there. This is the crux of it. This is the key. We have to go in.'

'It could have detonated a bomb,' said Kirsten. 'But it could also have sent a signal. People will come. The door's open. They check on these things, you know.'

'You can go,' Clarissa said to Kirsten. 'I'm going in there. I need to know what this is. And you aren't going to stop me.'

Chapter 15

'It's a risk,' said Kirsten.

'It's a risk we have to take,' said Clarissa. 'Macleod sent us to find out about the knife. He needs to know what's going on behind all of this. There are too many dead. Too many. Look, I'm scared. I'm absolutely petrified, but I need to know. You can run down there and have a look, but it'll mean nothing. It's why I'm here. It's why I've gone through this.'

Kirsten, meanwhile, was searching the man's body. She pulled out a mobile phone and broke it, before making sure that he was unconscious.

'Is he all right lying there?' asked Patterson. 'He's not going to wake up, is he?'

'No, he will not wake up,' said Kirsten. 'We have to be quick. Down the corridor! Go in and see what's down there, but be careful.'

'Don't you want to go first?' said Clarissa.

'I'm going to scout around back here,' said Kirsten. 'Make sure nobody's following us. Go in, go carefully. I'll be with you before you know it.'

Kirsten watched Clarissa and Patterson enter by stepping over the remains of the door that now lay on the ground. As soon as they were inside, she walked up the corridor. She looked left and right, before kneeling down the unconscious man on the floor.

Kirsten snapped his neck. It was quick; it was efficient, like she knew how to do. She dumped his body inside the large cabinet nearby. She wouldn't speak of it to Clarissa or to Patterson. Best they didn't know.

Besides, this man wasn't some security guard. He had no ID on him, nothing to say he was from the museum or to do with the tunnel structure. After picking up the bloody ritual knife Clarissa had used, Kirsten strode down the corridor. She found Patterson and Clarissa creeping along, the torch shining the way in front of them.

'Are we okay behind?' asked Patterson.

'We're good, Eric. Keep going,' said Kirsten.

Clarissa was up front now, half staggering, the torch swinging wildly. The tunnel was rough, and it bent round, here and there. It felt like they were going down, deeper into the ground.

And then, without warning, it opened out. Clarissa stood, illuminating the area bit by bit with the torch.

'Give me that a minute,' said Kirsten. She took the torch off Clarissa, pulled at it, and instead of having a direct beam out the front, it shone out on all sides. She placed it in the middle of the floor. Before them was a cavern. It was wide, and there were definitely shadows in the corner. The entire area had been dug out. At least that's what it looked like.

'Look at this,' said Clarissa. No longer was she a staggering woman, but had become an animated child. 'Stones. Central stone here. Other stones. Paintings on the wall. Pats, get your mobile. Get photographs of all those paintings. Everything.

CHAPTER 15

Then start photographing the area. Stick something down for measurement. Size. A shoe or something.'

'You need to be quick,' said Kirsten.

'We'll be quick as we can,' said Clarissa. She knelt down beside some stones. There were images on them.

'Pat, get the pictures.'

'Clarissa,' said Patterson, 'come over here.' He was beside one of the stones. 'This image,' he said, 'is it the same as the knife?'

The knife, thought Clarissa. *It was still back out there. She dropped it, she had . . .*

Kirsten came and handed over the knife. 'Got to keep your head at all times,' she said. 'Yes, you left it.'

Clarissa shook her head for a moment, but then, in the torchlight, held the knife up beside the image on the stone. It was the same.

'Look, Pats,' said Clarissa. 'Circle. It's a circle. The one in the middle. That stone is lower. Yes? You would sit on that, wouldn't you?'

'You could do.'

'It's a circle where they watch,' continued Clarissa. 'This is not quite an arena, but a . . . yes, it's a circle. It's a circle of people on the outside. Would you sit on those stones, or would you stand?'

'Some of the stones aren't complete, are they?' said Patterson.

It was true. There were some that were well-rounded; others were not so.

'But you watch the middle. Keep taking the pictures, Pats' said Clarissa.

'We need to move along,' said Kirsten. 'I mean it. We really need to go.'

But Clarissa was standing off to one side now, looking around. 'They killed them by slashing their throat. If they were sitting on that middle one, you could stand behind them and slash their throat. This could be it. This could be ritual based. It's very scary.'

'There's imagery on here. I think it's Norse. Northern European,' said Patterson.

'How do you know it's Northern European?' said Clarissa, marching up to him. She looked at it. 'It's Northern European. You have been reading those books, haven't you?'

'I try,' said Patterson.

'We really need to be going soon,' said Kirsten. She was looking down at her watch, but she didn't need to. There was a mental clock ticking in her head. *Signal goes off to get here. How quick could she get here? Five, ten minutes. Fifteen, twenty at most. Move in slowly to work out what's going on. Just in case you're running into a sizeable crowd.*

'Pats, look at this one. That's a knife. There's a picture of the knife. And this guy here, this guy is—photograph that guy . . . and photograph the image. I know him,' said Clarissa. 'I know him, I just can't think who he is.'

'I'm calling this. We need to go,' said Kirsten.

'No, you're not. I haven't got everything yet.'

'Then pick up a mobile yourself and photograph it,' said Kirsten. 'Stop standing and gawking at it. We haven't time.'

'Just watch the tunnel,' snapped Clarissa. She joined Patterson though, both photographing the entire area. As soon as she thought she had a full record of the place, she turned and walked over to the torch.

Clarissa picked it up and brought it back over to Kirsten,

CHAPTER 15

unsure how to collapse the light from going around it back to a direct beam. Kirsten took it off her, made a snap change on the torch and handed it back. Clarissa swung the beam back over the dig site.

'This is it. Pats; this is what he was talking about. This is what he was hiding.'

'We need to go,' insisted Kirsten.

'Give a girl a moment,' said Clarissa. 'This is . . . well, this is a piece of history.'

Clarissa found her hand being grabbed, and she was pulled along the tunnel. Kirsten also took the torch off her, using the beam to guide them in the dark passage, racing all the way until they got back to where they'd broken in.

The metal door was still lying down flat. But they heard something. Kirsten held up her hand. She stepped out on top of the metal door, slowly, easily, working her way up towards where this small section of tunnel joined the main one.

As she got close to the end, she stopped completely. Kirsten didn't look back, but her hand was held up to make sure that the other two hadn't followed. She held her breath, watching for it. It was dark, so she'd have to make sure she saw it. The point of the gun came round the corner first, and Kirsten pulled it hard, and a man followed.

She swung him brutally to bounce him off the wall, the gun falling from his hands. He gasped, and Kirsten was tempted to follow up, but waited, and then thanked herself that she did so, as another man came round the corner. She planted him up against the other wall.

'Who are they?' asked Clarissa, looking at the two collapsed men.

'Could they be guards?' asked Patterson.

Kirsten, satisfied that she couldn't hear anyone else, dropped and searched the men. There was no ID but there were guns and there were knives. There were mobile phones, too.

'We set the alarm off, and we disabled the bomb. In fact, because we set the bomb off, more likely, is why they are here. Or because we activated the door. There'll be more coming.'

'Did you—?' asked Clarissa.

'They were coming round that corner to empty their guns into my guts and yours,' said Kirsten. 'My world's different, okay? So kindly don't judge. I'm here for your safety. You're safe.'

Kirsten could hear heavy breathing behind her. Clarissa was clearly struggling with this reality. It was a good job she hadn't seen her despatch the man in the cupboard.

'We need to get out of here,' said Kirsten. 'Quick as we can.'

Together, they negotiated the tunnel, heading back up towards the entrance that they'd snuck in through. But Kirsten could hear someone outside the outer door.

'Back in,' she said.

They retreated carefully and Kirsten took them into the reception area, where they ducked down behind a desk.

'I need to secure a way out,' she said. 'Stay here. Don't come out. Do nothing! I will find you!'

'You're not leaving us,' said Clarissa. 'What if they come?'

'I'm leaving you to get you an exit,' said Kirsten. 'Trust me, I know what I'm doing. Stay quiet and don't move from here.'

Kirsten turned and disappeared off, leaving Clarissa and Patterson together. Clarissa was shaking.

'We'll get out,' said Patterson. 'We'll get out.'

'Stabbed him! I just stabbed him!' said Clarissa.

'He was killing you. You had to do it.'

CHAPTER 15

'He'll be dead now, won't he?' said Clarissa.

'You would have been dead if you didn't,' said Patterson. 'Come on, we've been through worse.'

'Worse?' whispered Clarissa.

'My neck, remember? They slashed my neck. You held it. You're tougher than this. Clarissa, you can do it.'

'I wouldn't have said it was worse,' said Clarissa. 'As bad, not worse.'

Patterson almost laughed but given the situation, he thought better of it. 'She knows what she's doing. Trust her. She trusted you. She let you go in and have your time in there. It was important and she let you make that decision. Now you have to let her decide about getting us out of here.'

Clarissa was trembling. Patterson wasn't sure if it was fright, nerves, or trauma, or just everything. He reached forward and hugged her. 'You're going to do good. Keep focused. Keep the brain going. Yes? We got the dig site. It's what we needed. We've got what we came for. We need to get out of here. So, let Kirsten get us out.'

'I wrote Frank a letter,' whispered Clarissa. 'I don't write letters. Pats, I had a bad feeling. I didn't think we were coming back.'

'And you let me come?' said Patterson.

Clarissa looked up into the balaclava clad face of Patterson. She could see the eyes beyond it. Patterson's eyes were always warm. 'Pats, I needed you with me. You do well, you know that.'

There was a voice behind them. 'I told you both to stay quiet.' A hand came down on both their shoulders. 'We're going to walk, and you will not say or do anything except walk. You're going to see some things, but you will ignore them, and you will focus on my feet ahead of you and getting out. Okay?'

Patterson nodded. So did Clarissa.

'You're doing good. You're doing good, girl. Come on.'

Clarissa stood up. *Girl? Did she just call me girl?* But she followed Kirsten's footsteps.

They turned past the reception, down to the staff quarters. Clarissa had to step over two bodies. She ignored the blood on either side until they'd walked out into the night. It was windy and cool, but the cold she was feeling may have come from the man lying on the ground. Somebody's neck shouldn't sit at that angle.

'Listen up,' said Kirsten, pulling them in beside a small hillock. 'I'm going to find somewhere to stash the pair of you. I'm then going to get everything together and we are getting the hell out of here.'

'Can we get something for her to eat?' asked Patterson.

'I wasn't aware I was doing catering as well,' said Kirsten.

'She's in shock,' said Patterson. 'Fluids and food. A chance to sit down.'

Kirsten looked around her and held out her hands. 'Doing the best I can,' she said. 'Under the circumstances, I don't think we should look to dine.'

Patterson rolled his shoulders.

'Come on,' said Kirsten. 'Time to get away from here.'

Chapter 16

'Are we going back to the apartment?' asked Patterson, wondering why they were so close to the town .

'No. We're not going anywhere near it. We were watched before. I need to get on top of what's happening first. I think I'll take you here.'

'Here?' said Patterson. 'Where's here?'

The trio had emerged from the centre and scouted round the far side of the island. Kirsten had slowly brought them closer until they were near some of the first buildings. They were all dark, but Kirsten was now approaching one. There were blinds drawn across the windows and across the entrance door. But otherwise, it looked like a normal restaurant.

'Why are we going in here?' asked Patterson. 'They won't be opening until later.'

Kirsten reached inside her clothing, and produced some pick locks. Soon she was inside, ushering the other two in. There was a bleeping sound, and Kirsten walked over to the wall, pulled out a device from inside her bag and slapped it onto a small electrical fixture. Soon the bleeping stopped.

'Was that their alarm?' asked Patterson.

'It was, but don't worry,' said Kirsten. 'These are dead easy to disable. The one we had to deal with back in the tunnels, an entirely different sort.' She went over and pulled out a chair and sat down at the table. 'The two of you, listen,' she said; 'don't remove any of your gloves or that. There's bound to be a bit of food about if you need it.'

'Where are you going to go?' asked Patterson.

'I told you, I need to see what's happening—if the heat's on, which I'm sure it will be. I won't be happy moving through the town with the two of you until I can see what's happening. However, if we can't go back to the apartment, I'll get in and I'll bring our stuff, okay?'

'And if we can go back?' asked Patterson.

'I'll put our stuff back in, and then I'll fetch you. But I don't see it. I think we've shaken the hornet's nest now.'

Kirsten disappeared back out of the door, telling them to lock it behind her. Patterson did so, but Clarissa simply sat at the table. Patterson got her a glass of water, which Clarissa drank slowly.

'Heads up,' said Patterson. 'Come on. I know it was dramatic. I know it was—'

'Shut up, Pats,' said Clarissa. 'I'm knackered, absolutely shattered. I had to jump that guy. He's taken it out of me. My whole back is bruised. He battered me off that wall.'

Patterson took her hand in his. 'And you're here, and we're alive. Kirsten's going to get us out of here. Okay? So, let's take it easy. She said wait here, so we wait here.'

'Wait here. Sit around. Do this. Do that. I'm not cut out for this, Pats. I'm an action person. You know that? Go in, raise merry hell.'

'Well, we raised merry hell, all right,' said Patterson. 'It's probably just what we didn't want to do.'

CHAPTER 16

'That guy, he didn't see my face.'

'I wouldn't worry about him,' said Patterson.

'Why, Pats?' asked Clarissa.

'You seriously think she'd have let them stay alive, having tangled with us? She's ex-Service. Their world's different. You don't leave loose ends. It's not the same as us.'

'You didn't have to tell me that,' said Clarissa.

About twenty minutes later, the door of the restaurant opened, causing them both to jump, but then they saw the sleek figure of Kirsten entering. She closed the door behind her and locked it before sitting down at the table.

'Well,' Kirsten said, 'the heat's really on now. There are people everywhere. Not in the open, but they're hiding; they're watching. They've got eyes on the apartment. Not just ours, but several others. So, they don't know it's us, but they're waiting to see.'

'But won't they go in and have a look?' said Patterson. 'I mean, early in the morning. Or if they don't see us down at breakfast.'

'By breakfast time, we won't be here. We're on the first ferry out of here,' said Kirsten. 'I'm going to get our stuff, and bring it back here. We'll sort ourselves from here, and then we'll make for the ferry. But we'll not go as a three to the ferry. You two will go separate to me.'

'You're meant to look after us,' said Clarissa. 'Kirsten, you're meant to be in charge of us, looking after us, the safety guru.'

'And I'm telling you, it's safer if you two go on your own. Don't worry, I'll be about. You won't see me. I'll see you, and I'll talk to you when I can. Once we get onto the German mainland, it'll be easier to go to ground, easier to get out. If all goes well, we'll be back up in Scotland in a couple of days.'

Kirsten stood up and made her way back outside, once again telling them to lock the door behind her. Patterson and Clarissa said very little, both thoroughly exhausted from what had happened that night. They were almost falling asleep when Kirsten opened the door again and came in.

'Right,' she said, 'here's the gear,' bringing in several smaller bags. 'We're going to have to do things differently.' She reached inside her own bag and produced a pair of clippers.

'What are those for?' asked Patterson.

'Going to change your hair slightly. You're going to go a bit shorter. Clarissa's going to go very short. In fact, it's all coming off.'

'What the hell do you mean it's all coming off?' said Clarissa, having to force herself not to shout.

'You two are going to go together, beloved son having brought his cancer-ridden mother over and now taking her away. I've got a scarf for you that you need to put on. The key thing is that you play it. Anybody comes near you, anybody makes a fuss, you play the cancer-ridden mother. It's all about you not being well. It's up to you, Patterson, to defend her under that ilk. I will stay aloof unless it looks like they're taking you somewhere, in which case I'll step in. But if it gets to that on this side of the water, we're in trouble.

'You haven't seen me go full tilt yet,' said Kirsten. 'If they pull you in, you'll see it. If that happens, there are no questions. You do exactly what I say. And you run.'

'Not sure I could run,' said Clarissa. 'You say this is necessary? All my hair? I've already dyed it grey for you.'

'You're not so old it won't grow back,' said Kirsten.

'Are you taking yours off, then?'

'No,' said Kirsten. 'I'm well used to changing my hair.

CHAPTER 16

More difficult to hide you, Clarissa. You're older. The skin, complexion. I can make myself look older. Can't make you look younger. Not going to work. Therefore, we have to change who you are completely.'

She took Clarissa and sat her down in a chair, and within the space of five minutes, had left Clarissa with an entirely bald head.

'I'm sorry. I don't have a mirror to show you.'

Clarissa looked up at her. 'If I find there was another way out of this, I will come for you.' Clarissa tried to raise a smile, but barely managed one before hopping over to sit down in her original seat, while Patterson took his place for a haircut. His was not so complete. Instead, Kirsten changed the angle of his hair, flipping the parting from one side to the other, and trimming up over his ears.

'It looks rubbish,' said Patterson afterwards.

'You look like a mother's boy,' said Kirsten. 'You've got to make it all about her. You've got to act. I know you can act. You need to do it.'

'And me,' said Clarissa.

'You just be a grumpy old bitch,' said Kirsten. 'Won't be a problem.'

Clarissa glared at her and then extended a digit up to show her displeasure.

Kirsten smiled. 'That's the fighting spirit.' Kirsten sat down, planning how to get off the island.

It was close to five in the morning when the trio left the restaurant after they'd tidied everything up. Kirsten was now sporting a red wig. Clarissa, with a scarf around her head, went arm in arm with Patterson. At first, they hurried out and around the town, before approaching the port more slowly.

The first departing ferry was at half-past six, and they arrived close to six o'clock. Kirsten was at a distance, chewing gum and watching through sunglasses. She had a bright skirt on. Clarissa thought about how Kirsten hadn't worn a skirt so far. It looked loose though, probably so she could still kick hard. She tried not to look over at Kirsten, as Patterson and she made their way towards the terminal. It was small, but there were a few people already gathering.

As they walked down, Clarissa could see someone walking towards them. There was a man in a suit, and he looked quite brusque. As she hobbled on along beside Patterson, she thought the man would step to one side, clear of her, but he didn't. Instead, he walked on, and his shoulder caught hers, sending her spinning to the floor. She hit it hard, crying out, and heard Patterson behind her. 'What on earth? How dare you, sir!' he said.

Patterson knelt down quickly beside Clarissa. His hand grabbed the top of her scarf. He pulled it, allowing it to fall away from her head. He reached down, hauling her up to her feet, and looked at the man who had turned, gazing at them.

'How many months of chemo? And you just march into her like that. Not even an apology. I don't care what language you speak, sir. Not a single apology. You will apologise to my mother.'

Although Clarissa was now up on her feet, Patterson made sure she was steady before stepping in front of her. The man looked him up and down.

'Anybody here speak German? Does anyone speak German?' said Patterson in a loud voice. 'Because I'm not having this. I'm not having it at all.'

A woman stepped forward. 'Yes, I speak German.'

CHAPTER 16

'Then tell this clown,' said Patterson, 'tell this clown that he has injured my mother and I demand an apology. She has cancer. Do you understand? Cancer. That's why she's got no hair. She was here on a trip, here for our last chance to see somewhere. And he—that man—he just barged into her.'

Patterson continued his rant while the woman translated. The man remained impassive before him. And then, Clarissa hobbled round the side of Patterson. She stood directly in front of the man, glaring into his eyes. 'What sort of a place is this?' said Clarissa.

'Mother, it's not good for you. Come on, come back. It's not good for you to be stressed like this. It's not.'

Clarissa swung her hand up and slapped the man hard across the cheek. It came from nowhere. She had deliberately waited, looking for him to be off guard. And when she hit him, it left a red mark on his cheek.

'Mother!' Patterson pulled her back.

'But he won't speak. He deserved it.'

'My sincerest apologies,' said the slapped man. He then turned and walked away.

Patterson turned Clarissa around and got her to walk over to where the tickets were being collected. He left her there while purchasing a couple at the nearby kiosk, before joining her and taking her onto the ferry.

It wasn't a large ferry, only a few decks, but Patterson went outside with Clarissa, who had the scarf tied back up on her head. They stood watching as Heligoland disappeared.

Patterson could breathe a sigh of relief. Clarissa too. But they weren't out of it yet. They were just away from that island. The sky was still dark, the fingers of dawn only beginning to take a true hold on the day. Patterson kept his arm tight on

Clarissa as they watched.

'I'm glad we're getting away from that place,' Clarissa whispered to him.

'Do you feel it?' said Patterson.

'Feel what?' asked Clarissa.

'The energy sapping away. The adrenaline dropping. I've just about kept going. I hope the trip home is quiet, relaxing.'

'I won't be happy till we are home,' said Clarissa.

'I think you actually did it, Patterson. I think we pulled it off. Terrific effort.' Kirsten had glided up behind them.

'Are we safe yet?' asked Clarissa.

'Safer,' said Kirsten. 'You must understand in this game, safe is a relative term. You are safer. Hopefully, in a couple of days, we'll be safer still in Scotland.'

'What do you mean, hopefully?' said Clarissa.

'Hopefully will do,' said Patterson. 'We got what we came for. Let's not bicker.'

Clarissa looked up at him, almost annoyed with the petulant attitude, and saw Kirsten looking over him in the same fashion. The man had a slight smile on his face. They'd come through. He was right. They'd come through.

Chapter 17

Macleod wasn't used to sneaking around. He'd done some of it in Italy, but so far in going to Clarissa's house, he'd arrived during regular hours. Yes, he was there for a different reason, because Clarissa hadn't been ill, and had been gallivanting around Europe. However, this time was different. Macleod was approaching the house at close to half two in the morning.

He'd received instruction from Kirsten that they'd be at the house that night, or rather, that morning, in the early hours. Frank didn't know this, and Macleod was going to wake him up to prepare for the arrival of his team. In truth, he was happy. Yet, as he crept along the streets, keeping out of the streetlights and approaching the neighbours of Clarissa, he was worried just how well he was doing with this covert action.

He crept up the driveway of the house behind Clarissa's, stole over a fence, or rather, hiked himself up to the top of it and fell down the other side. He then calmly made his way to the back door of Clarissa's house, for which he had a key. It was only when he stood on the back doorstep he realised there was someone watching him from the corner of the house. At first, he startled, but then she spoke.

'Don't worry,' she said. 'You haven't been spotted.'

The woman was a redhead and Macleod reckoned she was the one who had passed the house when he had looked out of the window with Perry. Anna Hunt's person, they had decided.

'How long have you been watching me?'

'Saw you arrive several streets away,' said the woman. 'Kind of figured where you were heading for, so came round the front and in. But you haven't been followed. There's no one else here. You're okay to go in. Though I wonder why you're going in at this hour.'

'If I refuse to answer, is that a problem?'

'I'll know anyway,' said the woman.

'I'd observe more than anything else,' said Macleod. And the woman nodded. He took out his key, opened the rear door, and stepped inside Clarissa's kitchen. Macleod made his way up the stairs, knocked gently on Frank's bedroom before stepping inside.

Frank awoke with a start.

'Don't put the light on,' said Macleod.

'Bloody hell, Seoras,' said Frank. 'I thought it was somebody coming for me. I thought it was—'

'You're being well looked after. There was a woman outside, I'm sorry to say who intercepted me, but knowing who I am, she let me go. You're being watched over, Frank. I wouldn't worry about it.'

'Well, why are you here?' he asked.

'She's on her way home. She'll be here shortly.'

Macleod saw the delight across Frank's face, and he went to get up and change.

'No, no. Just in case you're seen from a window or that. Be in your pyjamas. Put your dressing gown on if you want. But

CHAPTER 17

we'll not put the lights on until they get here.

Okay? I also can't be seen. Unlike previous times, I'm not meant to be here in the middle of the night.'

'I get you.'

'Have you got a room we can close off completely? So no light will leak out?'

'Not really,' said Frank. 'We build rooms with windows.'

Macleod laughed. 'Of course you do, but do you have a loft or—'

'Loft conversion up top? Is that what you're thinking?'

'Is it big?' asked Macleod.

'You might have to hold your head down, but you'll get everybody up into it.'

'That's where we'll go then.'

Macleod made his way back downstairs and into the kitchen. He sat waiting, pensive, wondering just what the news would be. And then he saw the kitchen door open. The black jeans were the first thing he saw, then the leather jacket, the long, thick black hair, and finally the smile.

Macleod stood up and walked over, but Kirsten, rather than embrace him, stepped back, allowing Clarissa and Patterson to enter. Clarissa still had a scarf around her head, and Patterson was sporting a rather strange moustache.

'I'm actually glad to see you,' said Clarissa. 'Where's Frank?'

'Shush,' said Kirsten. She closed the door behind her, locking it. She walked through the kitchen, checked the hallway, and then indicated they all should make their way upstairs.

'Frank's up in the loft. Apparently you've got an area up there, extension.'

'More like some floorboards,' said Clarissa. 'It's pretty steep up into it.'

Macleod watched as the three of them went ahead of her. And then Kirsten made her way up the stepladder that led into the loft before she made her way back down.

She turned to Clarissa. 'Off you go. I take it you don't need a hand?'

Clarissa glared at her and then took the scarf off her head. Macleod almost gasped at seeing her bald head. Clarissa made her way up, and the other three remained on the landing. There was a gasp above and then there were tears.

'I take it you met our friend outside?' said Macleod.

'Saw her. Fortunately, she didn't react.'

'I warned her you were coming. One of Anna's lot?'

'Yes,' said Kirsten. 'Sylvie's not bad. Good one for here. Wouldn't really send her overseas. Not sharp enough.'

'You okay, Patterson?' asked Macleod.

'We're home. We've got something we needed to get. Beyond that, I'm not sure I want to talk much about it.'

Macleod raised his eyebrow and looked at Kirsten. She simply shrugged her shoulders. 'It was rough,' she said. 'Well, for them it was rough.'

Macleod gave a little cough and then began climbing the stepladder up into the loft. He was followed by Patterson and Kirsten.

'Bit of a shock, isn't it?' Frank said to Macleod, nodding at Clarissa's bald head.

'I'm sorry,' said Kirsten. 'I did it to get us out. I will not go into any more detail. Her hair will grow. I'll have a wig here for her today.'

'Where do we do the debrief?' asked Macleod.

'We can do it up here,' said Clarissa.

'Clarissa, I'm grateful you came out, but I am not sitting

CHAPTER 17

talking to you now,' said Kirsten. 'Why don't you and Frank go down to the bedroom and just take the night? See you in the morning. She can't talk about a lot of things, Frank, but it was rough, so just—'

Clarissa took Frank's hand. 'He knows, and he knows we'll be fine.' Clarissa descended the loft ladder.

Macleod thought he could see a deep worry on Frank's face. Once they left, Macleod turned to Patterson. 'Why don't you crash in one of the other rooms? I'll talk to you tomorrow. You must be exhausted.'

'If you need a debrief, I can do it.'

'I need to talk to Kirsten. Other than that, everything can wait till the morning.'

Patterson nodded and made his way out of the loft. Kirsten turned to Macleod.

'They found it. They found the dig site. Lots of photographs. It was under the ground. Obviously, it had been there long before, but it had been found at some point by someone. Clarissa's saying that it's old. Older than the tunnels. She's going to have a look at it and get to the bottom of it. She hasn't much of a chance. We've been ducking here and there on the way back up.'

'People tailing?' asked Macleod.

'Not particularly. Just having to watch. Getting off the island was the hardest bit. Your Patterson boy's some actor.'

'And what about you? Did you cope with her?'

'You're going to have to watch Clarissa,' said Kirsten. 'There was an incident. I had to defuse a bomb, or a booby trap. Clarissa had to take someone on in a fight. He nearly killed her. She ended up stabbing him. She thinks he's back there somewhere. I couldn't let him live. Nobody back there who got close to us is alive. Those who think they saw us, well, maybe they'll have faces, but we're not there. We were disguised walking about, but the people that seem to run this, I think they're cleverer than that. What I can tell you is, I think you've kicked a veritable hornet's nest with this one,' said Kirsten.

'We shall see,' said Macleod. 'You should get some rest too, though.' He stepped forward, and the two of them embraced, holding each other tightly. 'It's good to see you back,' he said, 'and thank you for bringing them back. There's nobody else I would trust.'

'Get her to work tomorrow. See how good she is tracking this down.'

Macleod had an escort back to his car, the red-headed woman who'd been outside. Macleod drove home, spent the night with Jane, and then went to visit Clarissa's house the next morning.

He found her up in the loft area, along with Patterson. Frank had been relegated downstairs again, but Macleod thought that wasn't a bad thing. That's where he'd been for the previous week, moping about, pottering about here and there in the house, as if he was looking after her.

'How are we all this morning?' asked Macleod as he climbed the ladder up into the loft area.

It was tight enough, but Macleod was glad to see there was a pot of coffee sitting there. Kirsten poured him some, but she had a serious look on her face.

'Heligoland, sir,' said Patterson. 'There's been a report of a break-in and vandalism in one of the tunnels, but nothing else. Considering what happened, the amount of'—he stopped for a moment looking at Clarissa and then back to Macleod—'bodies that were there, it should have been big news.'

CHAPTER 17

'Showing you the control these people have. Even if they got a clean-up crew in,' said Kirsten, 'to keep it that quiet, to keep it under wraps. The place was buzzing once we'd been in.'

'Have we got anything else?' asked Macleod.

'I've been going through the photographs,' said Clarissa. 'There's something here. Forseti.'

'Forseti?'

'Yes, Forseti. I've called Sabine to come in and help deal with this, as Pats isn't up to it. We're going to have to go deep and we're going to have to be clever. The other problem we've got with the dig site,' said Clarissa, 'was there were no relics. There were paintings on the wall. We've got photographs of them. We've got the same symbol that's on the knife. So, the knife could have come from there, but there's nothing else. We have a stone circle, which looks like places for people to either sit or stand at, and there's one in the middle. The one in the middle looks like it's for sitting on. Or, it's a marker to hold people to. A place to watch in the round. It could be an execution pit, somewhere where everyone can see it. It's hard to say.'

'What's the time period?'

'Frisian. From the Frisian people up north. It looks like, well, old northern mythology. That's where Forseti comes from. Norse god to put things right. *The presiding one.* Not that clued up on him. In fact, I've only just recognised the character but we'll get somewhere.'

'You'll have to explain it all to me at some point. I need to understand the mind of these people.'

'Of course. First and foremost, we need to find the character. We need to find any artwork that deals with him. Any deals, any artwork, any artifacts. I'm wondering was the dig site looted, and these people had to go looking for the artefacts?

If you had all the artifacts from the dig, you could just keep them there? The place was well secured,' said Clarissa.

'They actually kept it secret by putting a metal door in and saying that the tunnels beyond had collapsed,' said Kirsten. 'Very clever. When you opened the door, they still had a false door to the rougher tunnel beyond. It looked like there'd been the cave in. There was nowhere for the tunnel to go. When you got through that door, there was then a booby trap with a bomb. After that, you got to the dig site. That would have been secured enough for artefacts. I don't know what else they could have done,' said Clarissa. 'It was out of sight. Well hidden.'

'But you found it,' said Macleod. 'Not hidden enough.'

'I think the artefacts have been on the move. If they wanted one knife, they'll want more. I'm treating them as cultists, religious fanatics or near as, dammit. So, we chase up the Forseti character and see if we can find anything.'

Sabine arrived later on that day and Macleod disappeared for a bit. He returned later in the evening, back to the loft. Kirsten was sitting down again, legs crossed in the corner. He wondered if she'd been there all day. Clarissa and Sabine were sitting in front of the laptop, Patterson looking on from behind.

'Sabine found it, Seoras. We've got Forseti's name mentioned in some private auctions. There seems to be a common name with the auctions. Don't know how heavily he's involved,' said Sabine, 'but from what I'm reading, he's certainly at the centre of the auctions. We may be able to go there and find receipts. He has to say who he sold them on to. Public record of the auctions even if they were closed.'

'Not a private one?' said Macleod. 'I thought they did private ones.'

'No, this was closed, so private in that you need an invitation but the sale is disclosed in the public domain. The trouble with private ones,' said Clarissa, 'is people wonder what you're buying. People like me look at them closely. These items have come out, and they're not worth mega money, but they may be priceless in a religious sense to these people. But they're not worth mega money, so therefore, buy them openly. Nobody's going to get overexcited. Forseti's not a weird character, in that sense. There's no association of him and murderous cults, but he's definitely involved. He's the core figure in all of this.'

'We need to get the low-down on these auctions,' said Patterson.

'Pats is right. It's where we need to be. The arts team need to be on top of this.'

'No, they don't,' said Macleod. 'You've done a great job for us, but at the moment, you need to be here recovering,' said Macleod. 'We can't blow that cover.' He looked across at Kirsten. She nodded.

'No,' she said, 'too early.'

'I can't send you either, Sabine,' said Macleod. 'You're known. I could ask Kirsten to go, but—'

Kirsten interrupted him. 'I don't know what I'm looking for, and I don't have a clue about it.'

'Pats is too green for it too,' said Clarissa.

'And may have been spotted in Heligoland,' said Macleod.

'So what do we do then?' asked Sabine.

Macleod thought for a moment, then he gave a smile. 'I've got an idea,' he said. 'I'm not sure it's going to work, but I've got an idea.'

Chapter 18

'Is this one all right? Does it say power dressing? Does it say new?'

Kirsten looked over at Tanya. The woman had come all the way up from Glasgow to be Macleod's personal assistant, and yet her first job was to go on a stakeout for him. She had a trim figure, and despite her age, she looked in good shape to Kirsten. Kirsten had noticed that if people were going to let their figure go, often it was when they got to forty something.

In your youth, a lot of your time was kept for you, even if you were busy running around. Then kids, families, and other things got more and more involved. You seemed to slow down, do less. Kirsten, of course, worked out. She had to for her job. Or what had been her job. Not being in shape could get you killed.

She watched as Tanya buttoned up a blouse, but stopped lower down than Kirsten would have.

'You can see the top of the bra,' said Kirsten.

'It's the whole point, isn't it?' said Tanya. 'I'm bait.'

'Come over here a minute,' said Kirsten, and she pressed a small device inside of Tanya's ear. She then reached down inside her blouse, sorting out a microphone into the collar.

CHAPTER 18

Kirsten stepped back. She couldn't see anything. She walked over to the wall of the hotel room and banged on it twice. Sitting next door was Clarissa, along with Ross.

'So you should hear Clarissa, in a minute. Ross and she have got a screen. They can see everything through the camera, just to the side of your blouse. What you can't do is let him open that blouse.'

'How close am I going to get to this guy?' asked Tanya. 'I was told to flirt a little with him. I don't have to go—'

'You can't go,' said Kirsten. 'You need to make sure he doesn't open that blouse any further. If he does, he'll see wires. It'll blow your cover. You'll have your chauffeur in with you,' said Kirsten. 'He's also wired up to Clarissa.'

'One, two, one, two. Hello? Can you hear this? Anyone hear this? Are you sure this is bloody working, Ross?'

Tanya shook her head. Clarissa was loud. 'I can hear you,' she said. 'I can hear you loud and clear. In fact, very loud. Can we turn it down a touch? Ross, can you turn it down a touch? She has a very loud voice.'

'Don't incline your head,' said Kirsten. 'Whenever you hear a voice, don't incline your head. It's only in one ear. So don't incline your head towards it.'

'Okay, okay,' said Tanya. Tanya turned back to the mirror and pulled the blouse down before she put on a small jacket. She reached and took a comb and brushed her blonde hair back. It wasn't as thick as twenty years ago, but it was doing okay. She smiled at herself in the mirror.

'Are you okay?' asked Kirsten.

'I think so. I just engage him?'

'Listen to Clarissa's instructions. She'll feed you information. If you're looking at any art, she'll see what you're looking at. If you pick something up, hold it like this,' said Kirsten, putting her hand out approximately ten inches from her own chest. 'That means it looks like you're studying it, but Clarissa will see it on the camera.'

Tanya took her brush and held it ten inches from her own chest. 'Clarissa?' she said.

'Yes, I'm here.'

'The brush in my hand. Can you see it clearly?'

'Yes, that's fine.'

Tanya nodded and put down the brush. 'We're good then. I just wish Perry was here. Macleod's not here either.'

'No,' said Kirsten. 'I know you don't know me. This is the first time we've met, but I do this. This is what I do, and that's why I'm here. Macleod can't be seen near us. He has to be doing his normal functions. Clarissa's meant to be in a house at the moment, getting better. And the rest of the team? Well, we're just off and about doing our normal work.'

'I appreciate that. I just wish Perry was about.'

There was a knock on the hotel room door. Kirsten went over, looked through the peephole, then opened it, allowing Clarissa to march in. She was wearing a rather demure pair of trousers and a blouse. She had a blonde wig on as well.

'You ready?' she said, and Tanya nodded. She turned and Clarissa looked at her full length. 'Blimey. Well, you should catch his attention anyway. Just be careful. Don't let him get too close. If he's looking for anything beyond a bit of close company, if he moves over to slap and tickle . . . well then, get yourself out of there.'

'Slap and tickle?'

'I think she means if he makes sexual advances—i.e., if he starts to try to remove clothing,' said Kirsten.

CHAPTER 18

'Slap and tickle,' said Clarissa. She stared at the other two women, and then told them she'd be next door as it was time to get moving. She wished Tanya good luck and left.

'You'll see Patterson on the street,' said Kirsten, 'but maybe you won't. I've got him out there keeping an eye. If things go wrong, he can move in and distract the man, get you away. But you've also got your chauffeur there for protection.'

'I hope this works. I'll see what I can find out.'

Tanya made her way downstairs, out of the hotel, to a BMW that was sitting on the street outside. As she approached it, the driver stepped out, dressed in a smart chauffeur's outfit, but with a large beard and a rather rotund belly. She gave him a nod and in a rather gruff voice, he said, 'Ma'am,' and opened the rear door for her. Tanya clambered in. She was nervous, and the chauffeur said nothing as he got into the front seat and drove off. Maybe that was for the best. He was there for protection, after all.

They arrived outside an art studio in the depths of Edinburgh. It wasn't quite where the tourists went, but it wasn't far off that track and was located at the bottom of a tall building. You had to go down the side and in via an entry, but once inside, it looked fairly sumptuous.

Pieces of artwork were displayed here and there, portraits on the walls with other paintings. As Tanya glided in, she was met by a man who was at least six feet in height, although he had all the width of a postage stamp. He was tall and thin, but one thing he had were eyes that could stare. Tanya watched as his eyes dropped from her face, down, and then back up before descending again.

'You must be Miss Oxenby. Delighted to meet you. My name's Michaels. I think we may have some items you would enjoy. Champagne?'

'I know what he's looking at,' said a voice in Tanya's ear. It was Clarissa. And then she could hear another voice, slightly more hushed, as if it was at a distance from the microphone.

'She can hear every word you say.' Tanya guessed it was Ross. But she'd never really spoken to him, so she wasn't sure.

'Let him take you to show you some of the art.'

Tanya's hand was taken by Michaels and he approached a portrait on the wall. He started waxing lyrical about this eighteenth-century item but Tanya could hear a voice in the background.

'Correct him. Seventeenth. Tell him late seventeenth.'

'I think you'll find, Mr Michaels, That portrait is the late seventeenth century.'

'There should be a little card down below it. Most artwork is labelled when you go into studios. He's removed it. He's testing you,' said Clarissa.

'Oh my, my. You're correct, of course,' said Michaels. 'Not just a . . . a beautiful specimen, but also—'

'Also what?' said Tanya. 'You're surprised to find a woman like me with a brain?'

'You're a work of art indeed,' said Michaels. His hand went up to her shoulder.

'Don't flinch,' said Clarissa. 'He's interested. Keep him interested.'

'What else have you got for me, Mr Michaels?' said Tanya.

She turned her head, almost flashing her eyes at him. Tanya tried to be subtle, thinking about how she would lure a man on, at least one she liked. She continued to flirt with him. Every now and again she would glance at her chauffeur, who, having come inside the art studio, was standing off to one side. His

CHAPTER 18

hands were clasped in front of him, but behind the big thick beard, his eyes were penetrating, watching everything she did.

'Take him across to the paintings on the far right,' said Clarissa. 'Don't let him speak. We're going to tell him all about it, all of them, and we're going to tell him we're interested in more of them.'

Tanya took the man's hand and led him across. Following Clarissa's prompting, she detailed each picture, exactly where it had come from, what it was, and how she felt about it. Tanya had no idea what Clarissa was saying, but Clarissa fed through the information in such an impassioned way, it was easy to pick up the intonation.

'Do you have anything more?' said Tanya, following Clarissa's prompting. 'Something of a bit more value, something more special?'

'I do,' said the man. 'Let me get you something to drink.' He disappeared and came back with a bottle of champagne, opening it with dramatic effect before pouring a glass for Tanya. 'This way,' the man said.

Tanya walked with him until he got to two doors. One was sitting open and had desks beyond it, but one was distinctly locked. 'It'll be just through here,' said Michaels. He covered up a keypad, pressed buttons, and opened up the door into another room. As he did so, warm lights came on inside, and he stood at the door smiling. 'Maybe we'll leave your chauffeur outside.'

'I go where she goes,' said the chauffeur.

'Tell the chauffeur no,' said Clarissa in the earpiece. 'Be forceful.'

'I don't need you at the moment,' said Tanya, waving a hand at her chauffeur, but a little unsure of what Clarissa was playing at. This door had a keypad on it, did it not?

Tanya stepped inside. She could almost feel the anger from her chauffeur.

'You stay there, Mr Chauffeur,' said Michaels and the door closed behind her. As Tanya walked into the special collection, her heart was thumping. She felt a hand running down her back. He was actually caressing her backside. *What a leach*, she thought. But instead, she breathed in deeply and smiled at the man as if she was enjoying it.

* * *

'Right, Perry, get in the office.' Perry heard Clarissa's forceful voice in his ear. The large beard he was wearing was tickling him, and he was quite concerned that Tanya had disappeared off on her own into the special collections. On the bright side, he knew Clarissa was watching everything on Tanya's camera, as well as the camera mounted on his own clothing. Patterson was outside, and Kirsten wasn't that far away, either. If things were going south, she could come in and assist. But, at the moment, by the tone of Clarissa's voice, things were going swimmingly.

Perry went into the office of Michaels. Michaels had obviously been alone within the studio, and had wanted to greet Miss Oxenby, as Tanya was portraying. And possibly, he wanted a delightful time with her. According to Clarissa, he had a reputation for it.

Perry pulled papers out from in front of him on the desk. Through Clarissa talking to him on 'chauffeur cam,' as she described it, he was directed to take photographs of different bits of paper. Using a device Perry shoved into the side of the

CHAPTER 18

desktop computer, Ross was able to use a program to hack out details from the computer.

It would take several minutes.

Perry thought about Tanya. This wasn't what he had thought about when she was coming up. He'd had to hold his breath when she came out to the BMW. She wasn't that sort of person. She didn't dress using her sex as a weapon. Although Perry couldn't deny the allure.

However, he kept focused. It took him a good five minutes to pull out most of the papers and take photographs. Clarissa was on to him constantly. *Look in here, check this, do that.* Eventually, he thought he had everything. He looked back, tidying everything up to where it had been, and took the little dongle out from the desktop, tucking it back inside his pocket.

'That's a wrap,' said Perry. 'Get her out of there.'

'Easy,' said Clarissa. 'Go back to where you were before and stand like you've been there the whole time.'

Perry returned, but this was worse, for now he was standing, doing nothing, and all he could think of was Tanya, a room away. He could hear the odd little laugh and giggle from her. That wasn't her. She didn't flirt like that.

***

'Mr Michaels, you really know how to treat a woman, don't you?' said Tanya. She drained a glass of champagne, putting it down, and moved over to another sculpture sat on a pedestal.

'I acquired this—' Michaels began.

'You acquired this in a rather dodgy auction because this hasn't been seen for several years. Am I right?' said Tanya, laughing.

'Spot on. You really know your stuff. It's quite something to see a woman who not only looks good but knows her business.'

His hand descended again, fondling her backside. She dropped her hand down his back and smacked him gently on his. 'Enough time for that later,' she said.

'Take me over to the two paintings on the far side of the room,' said Clarissa in Tanya's ear.

Tanya turned and pointed. 'Ooh, look at those,' she said, and marched off, Michaels desperately following her.

'Bloody hell,' said Clarissa. Tanya didn't know what to do with that. 'Get up close,' she said. 'Really close, far corner of the second one, down to the bottom left.'

Tanya leaned in, as if examining the middle of the painting, but the camera would have been close to edge of the painting.

'That's a fake,' said Clarissa. 'That's a fake. These are fakes. These three in the corner are fakes. Ask him about them.'

'Where did you pick these up from?' asked Tanya.

'I travelled abroad for those. I think it was Venice. Little dealer at the back. Of course, I got someone to check them for me. Make sure they were authentic. As you can see, the paperwork is beside them as well.'

Tanya moved over towards it, allowing the camera to glance across it.

'Point out the bottom left-hand corner to him. Tell him it's inconsistent. Then, go to the first picture. Go to the middle of it. Show the inconsistency around the farmhouse. Then, go to the third one. Tell him at the top, the top right is not consistent. The brush strokes are not the right direction. Then, slap him for giving you such rubbish and march out.'

Tanya did as instructed. She built up to it, though, getting herself into a rage. After decrying the third painting, she

CHAPTER 18

turned and delivered an almighty smack across the man's face with her open hand. Touch her backside, would he? As she strode across, she shoved her hand at a vase, knocking it to the floor.

'Most of it's bloody fake!' she shouted.

Tanya opened the door of the private collection, marching out. The vase she'd smacked had crashed onto the floor and broke into many pieces. As she got out, Michaels was running after her, but the chauffeur stepped across, standing in his way.

'Miss Oxenby is leaving,' he said. 'I wouldn't.'

Tanya turned and looked, and the chauffeur had his hand inside his jacket pocket. Michaels backed off, and Tanya gave her chauffeur a nod, and marched out. The chauffeur was quick behind her, opening the door to allow her into the BMW, before getting inside to drive off. As she sat back, she breathed out a sigh of relief. But there was a voice in her ear.

'The vase,' said Clarissa. 'I said nothing about the vase.'

'I thought it would look good for effect,' said Tanya.

'Oh, it looked good,' said Clarissa. 'Fifteen grand's worth, smashed to pieces. There was nothing fake about it.' Tanya gulped. 'Still, I'm not sure he would have known,' said Clarissa.

Chapter 19

The team had regathered at Clarissa's house approximately a day later. It was the early hours of the morning, the only time when Macleod could visit. He brought Tanya with him, feeling that she needed a better introduction to the team. She'd been whisked over once she'd agreed to do the Edinburgh job, and she didn't really know anyone. He'd brought her into something, and she needed to be aware of who she could trust. Having entered Clarissa's house from the rear, as was his usual clandestine method, he took Tanya up into the rather cramped loft conversion.

When there were only a few people up there, it was fine, but now most of the team had gathered. Clarissa was sitting alongside Patterson. Perry had also joined them. Kirsten was there, as well as Sabine. They'd obviously been working hard before Macleod's arrival. As he entered the loft, he was handed a cup of coffee.

'Perry said to me you're more of a tea person,' said Patterson, handing a cup to Tanya.

'Tea?' said Macleod. 'You never told me that. Can't have my secretary drinking tea.' And then he smiled.

'She can drink whatever she wants after that performance,'

said Perry.

Tanya looked over and smiled at him.

'Everyone, you probably know, but this is Tanya. She'll be my new PA, starting tomorrow. However, she's done a little bit of work for us, which you all know about. So, I felt she should meet the rest of the team. You've met Clarissa. Kirsten too,' said Macleod. 'This is Patterson. He was out on the street protecting you. Sabine there worked on the arts side with Clarissa for a long time. She now works with Detective Inspector Emmett Grump on cold cases. However, everything's connected at the moment. We're one enormous family. So just in case anything happens, these are faces you can run to.'

Perry handed over a couple of pictures to Macleod.

'And these people aren't here tonight because I can't bring everyone all the time to secret meetings,' said Macleod. 'But that's Emmett Grump. This is DI Hope McGrath. And that one is Susan Cunningham. The other one there is Yona Nakamura. Yona's forensic lead at the station. Yona can be trusted.'

'There's only one thing I don't understand,' said Tanya. 'Was one of them playing the chauffeur?'

'The chauffeur?' said Macleod. 'No, no, no. That's your chauffeur over there.' Tanya looked, and he was pointing at Perry.

'Didn't want to put you off,' said Perry. 'You did a great job. It's hard to act when you know the other individual personally, though. Especially to treat them abruptly. Thought it best you didn't know it was me.'

'You've got rid of the sexy beard,' said Tanya, laughing. 'And the podge.'

Perry looked a little embarrassed, and Macleod could see

the fondness.

'Been going through the receipts,' said Clarissa, 'and everything that was in the office with Pats and Sabine. Seoras, we seem to have receipts for a Mr Oliver and he's buying up anything that has Forseti on it. Michaels has dealt with several Forseti items and Oliver has bought them every time. And for exorbitant sums. It's no wonder he's running a studio like that if somebody's buying items for that sort of money.'

'Forseti?' asked Tanya.

'We're hunting down two different groups,' said Macleod. 'Forseti is a historical figure, or at least a mythological one, who seems to be important to one group. So, the artwork with Forseti associated with it that Michaels was selling might give us a link into the group. I don't think we'll say more than that to you. It's best you don't know everything.'

'Of course,' said Tanya. 'Do you want me to go?'

'No,' said Macleod. 'We trust you.'

'Come sit over here,' said Perry. 'I don't really do the art side either.'

He was sitting down on the floor because there were only a couple of seats in the loft conversion. Tanya moseyed over and sat down close to Perry, leaning into him.

Macleod saw her smile. He'd have to keep an eye on that. There was definite affection there.

'Any idea who Mr Oliver is? Is he a dealer people know? Is he a collector? What?' asked Macleod.

'Been looking into it,' said Sabine. 'Lemon and Light have been making some routine inquiries down around Glasgow. Nobody seems to know Mr Oliver. Can't find his name on other auctions, ones that are very open and legitimate. Very specific buyer, by the looks of it.'

CHAPTER 19

'When you say exorbitant sums,' asked Macleod, 'how exorbitant?'

'They're such,' said Clarissa, 'that nobody else would even bother to bid. Imagine if you wanted something, and you knew it was going to go for round about a certain price. If you doubled that, most people wouldn't bid at all, because they couldn't sell it on. You'd have to really want it. I mean really want it. Not as an investment. Oliver isn't investing by buying Forseti artifacts. He wants the artifacts for other reasons. At least, that's my take on it,' said Clarissa.

'I agree,' said Sabine.

'And me,' said Patterson.

Clarissa looked over at Patterson. 'I'm not sure you're qualified enough yet to make that call, Pats.'

'I know exactly what you've said. I know the values of the items. This isn't about the items. This is about people. I get it.'

'Anyway,' said Macleod, 'we've got a consensus. That's good. What can we do with it?'

'Well, if we can get ahead of the game, maybe we could spot him at an auction.'

'It's a nice idea, Pats,' said Clarissa, 'but these auctions have been private. Getting into them would be difficult. We want to stay under cover,' Clarissa said to Macleod. 'If we go in rattling feathers to try to get into a secret auction, it won't work. We'll blow the cover straight away. We must come at this from a different angle.'

'Such as?' asked Macleod.

'Well, maybe we can lure him in. We have got the sacrificial knife.'

'Sacrificial knife's our major piece of evidence.'

'No, it's not,' said Clarissa.

'Yes, it is,' said Macleod.

'We haven't even logged it. If you were to take that to court, how on earth would you explain. "Oh yes, Hope got off the boat and slipped the knife to Kirsten and oh, then we forgot about it and didn't register it and went halfway off around the world trying to sort something out?" That wouldn't work. It's not our primary source of evidence. It's our fundamental way into these people. The knife is a gift. The knife is something that says we have access if we wield it correctly.'

'I'm not just backing my boss up with this,' said Patterson, 'but Clarissa's right. Mr Oliver, from our investigations, doesn't seem to like the light. He's buying everything in secret auctions, not indulging in anything else. He keeps himself quiet for a collector.'

'What do you mean "for a collector?"' asked Clarissa.

Perry burst out laughing. Clarissa shot him a look.

'What he means,' said Perry, 'is it's not you.'

'I didn't say that,' said Patterson.

'Pats, explain yourself,' said Clarissa.

'Most collectors have a bit of flamboyance about them. You like to flaunt your knowledge,' said Patterson to Clarissa. 'You announce your presence. Until we went through this case, you would turn up in your tartan and trews for sure. Everybody knew Clarissa. She was the dealer. It's one of the biggest problems we've got when we go after people. They see you. They know what you're about.'

'Sabine's not like that though,' said Clarissa.

'Sabine's not a collector. She's not a dealer. Sabine's a police officer,' said Patterson.

'But she knows her art,' said Clarissa.

'She does, but she doesn't collect it and show it off like you

CHAPTER 19

would because she's not a true arts person. She likes it, but she's not there to tell the rest of the world about it. Very personal to Sabine,' said Patterson. He saw Sabine smile at him.

'Nobody's ever put it like that,' said Sabine. 'I've always thought myself different to Clarissa.'

'Well, you look pretty different,' said Tanya. 'What, twenty years, at least? Sabine also looks like almost ex-military. She's in good shape.'

'I am in excellent shape for my age, and this discussion is stopping now. It is not about the differences between me and Sabine,' said Clarissa. 'Your point, Pats.'

'My point is Mr Oliver is one of those quiet people. So, you are correct. We must bait him in. We will not find him but will have to lure him. A subtle difference, but an important one.'

Kirsten had been sitting in the corner quietly. She had this habit of not involving herself in the police discussions. Macleod thought it was because she was no longer an officer. But he also wondered if she was getting better at musing over things, letting other people throw the ideas up. But now she had rocked forward, off her bottom onto her knees, in the corner of the loft conversion.

'She's right,' Kirsten said. 'Look, we risked an awful lot. At the moment, to go after Oliver is all we've got. If we close off that route, if we go after him too noisily in the arts world, we lose everything. Clarissa says it's Forseti items being bought in private auctions, so we need to set up our own private auction and bait them in. That's what'll work. These people are fanatical about Forseti. They're not fanatical about art, like Clarissa.' Kirsten rocked back down onto her backside.

Macleod took a thoughtful sip of coffee. 'Okay,' said Macleod, 'how do we get it out there? How are you going to set up a private auction without stirring things up?'

'We can't put the knife out,' said Clarissa. 'Not on its own. That's too obvious. We need to come up with other items to do with Forseti.' She pondered for a moment, then looked over at Sabine. 'Icelandic? Do we go Icelandic? He's in their mythology. It would make sense.'

She turned back to Macleod. 'We get some Icelandic items. They can be similar to Forseti, but not specifically about Forseti. Forseti was only one god. We get these items, and we bring them together. Maybe put them into an auction at an auction house. Not just go for a private.'

'Like you said, private is difficult,' said Clarissa. 'But even if you're in private auctions, you'll still be looking around.'

'He may not buy the other ones directly,' said Sabine. 'Or he may follow items afterwards to buy. Of course, he may just buy them under a different name when he's doing it publicly.'

'Yes, Sabine, yes,' said Clarissa. 'We do a public auction first. Stick the knife into a public auction and see who comes for it. We get Icelandic items, mythological items with histories similar to what the knife would be, linked to those around Forseti. We then put the knife in the middle of it. Call it a collection somebody's selling off.'

'And that'll bring him out, will it?' asked Macleod.

'We can see,' said Clarissa. 'If it doesn't, so what? We'll just run a public auction.'

'If it's public, how are you going to run it?' asked Macleod. 'You can't be seen at it, can you? You can't be.'

'DS Lemon and DC Light. They're the ones we need.'

'They're your new recruits down in Glasgow, aren't they?' said Tanya. Everyone turned to look at her. 'Glasgow HR? I take it there was nothing under the radar about them because

CHAPTER 19

we got all the details.'

'I'd rather they weren't brought in,' said Macleod. 'We're dealing with people who kill quickly. There's enough of you at risk at the moment. I don't want there to be any more.'

'Why are they going to kill them? It's public. I'll tell them just to keep a low profile or to run it in such a way that they don't put themselves into harm,' said Clarissa.

'I would be very cautious in involving them,' said Macleod.

'Seoras,' said Clarissa. And then she stopped. 'Detective Chief Inspector. This is my field. I can keep them safe because I know how to run this. I know how to not make them look like they're involved. Remember, the knife wasn't put into evidence. The knife went down in the boat, as far as those from the Forseti group believe. That means this is a different knife. That means this is one of the set.'

'If it is a set,' said Macleod. 'You don't know it's a set.'

'It's a sacrificial knife,' said Sabine. 'It'll be one of a set. Very probably.'

Clarissa nodded to Sabine and turned back to Macleod. 'This is my investigation,' said Clarissa. 'And this is my decision. Yes?'

Macleod nodded slowly.

'Well, in that case,' said Clarissa, 'we set this up. Icelandic items into an auction with the knife and we see who turns up. We set the bait.'

'Sounds like a plan to me,' said Kirsten.

'Get it underway then,' said Macleod. 'Tanya, we'll get you home. Thank you for coming.'

Tanya stood up, along with Perry. She went to leave, but she turned round and kissed him on the cheek.

'Thanks for being there,' she said. 'See you in the office.'

She left the loft conversion along with Macleod, and Clarissa turned to look at Perry. 'Oh, aye,' she said. 'Or was it just the beard and the fake belly that got to her?'

Perry ignored the comment. He was simply staring at the ladder that led to the loft conversion. After a moment, he reached down and picked up the photographs that Macleod had left to one side. On the top of them was the picture of Susan Cunningham. It stopped him in his tracks for a moment. *Oh well, Perry boy*, he thought. *Let's just see what comes.*

Chapter 20

Sam Lemon buttoned up his shirt almost all the way to the top. He then undid a button. After all, he didn't want to look too formal. He then looked down at his shoes. There was a mark on the left one, so he reached down, wiping it off. He looked smart now. Very smart. He took his comb and brushed his short hair before gazing into the mirror. He looked good. And he was going to make a good job of this.

The call had come in from Clarissa. Or DI Urquhart. His boss. More than that, his new boss. She had asked little of him so far, but he got the feeling that this was important. He wasn't quite sure why, but it was up to him and his new colleague, Erin Light, to dig out some Icelandic folklore artifacts.

It had taken them over a week to get some, but Erin had quite the touch about her. She seemed to know the arts world inside out. Sam was quite a newcomer, and although he understood how things worked, Erin, at twenty-two, seemed to have more contacts than he ever had.

She explained to him that her father had been a dealer. She'd grown up her whole life with it, and her mother had been a police constable before she died. Now Erin was a detective working in the arts group.

She didn't look like a police officer. Erin was a big build of a girl. At least that's what Sam's mother would have called her. She had long blonde hair that more sort of hung around rather than was kept in place. And baggy jumpers that made you wonder if she was embarrassed by her shape. There was a sloppiness to the way she dressed. But, in fairness, not in the way she acted.

Yes, she seemed easy-going, but she was clever with it. Having gathered her Icelandic items, they'd made the journey north, stopping in a hotel just outside Inverness. His boss was still recovering in her house, and they'd visited. Clarissa had seemed delighted with the items they'd picked up, but she'd also given them another one and charged Sam with not losing it. This was when everything had changed.

He'd asked her about it, and she said it was from a character called Forseti. It was important that Forseti was linked into the blurb that the auction house booklet would produce. Sam was to make sure that it wasn't too prominent in the descriptions but was in with the rest of the Icelandic descriptions.

Erin wanted them put in as a group to secure a good deal, but no, Clarissa said she wanted them sold separately. And when they put them in, they were to go along to the viewing days and make a note of anyone who was looking particularly at the knife.

Erin had asked Clarissa about the value of the knife. Clarissa threw it back to her, and Erin thought you might get a couple of thousand for it. Clarissa agreed that was a sensible price, but warned that there may be somebody else bidding a lot more. It was key that whoever bid on the items was followed.

Today was the first day of viewing, and the auction would be in two days' time. Sam looked once again in the mirror,

CHAPTER 20

pulled at his shirt, partly wishing he had a tie on, then grabbed a rather suave jacket before stepping out of the hotel room. He took a left to the room next to him and knocked on the door. It was time to go.

'Hang on,' said a voice, and then a door opened slightly. 'You can come on in. Don't worry about it.'

Sam stepped in and could see a baggy jumper being put on by Erin. She had her back to him, but the jumper hadn't descended far enough, and he caught a view of the bra strap before the jumper fell down. Erin turned round, her hair swinging round her face, before she grabbed some boots. She had a long skirt on as well, and Sam thought she looked like a travelling person. Maybe someone who would have been with a circus in years gone by.

'I'm nearly there, Sam,' she said. 'I just need to brush this hair.' She seemed to attack it with gusto while Sam stood, rather embarrassingly, in the corner. He didn't come into the rooms of women. This wasn't a place he should be.

But for all that, he couldn't help but like Erin. Everybody couldn't help but like her. She smiled; she spoke well; she was always enthusiastic. Not that he had eyes on her. Beyond being a colleague, she would do his head in if he actually was in a house with her or had to share a place with her. He looked around her room.

Here and there were items of clothing or of make-up. She'd only been in here a day. How could a hotel room get this messy? But then he'd seen the case she'd brought. It was enormous. He always travelled in a way that you could jump on a flight with his case and not pay any extra. Erin seemed to travel like she was taking the entire circus with her.

It was another ten minutes before Erin stepped out with

him and they got into the car before driving out to the auction house inside Inverness. It looked like a load of farm sheds, with nothing particularly glamorous about it. Sam had set up inside his jacket a small camera that shot pictures with a touch of a button that he carried in his hand. On entering the premises, he didn't quite hover around the Icelandic items, instead drifting around, acting as if Erin was his daughter.

She would pick up items, look at them, but Sam would look distracted as if he shouldn't be there, but he was watching closely. Several people picked up the Icelandic items, and he passed by, taking photographs of them all. In truth, he must have had nearly fifty by the end of the day.

Leaving around five o'clock, the pair stopped off in a small pub for something to eat, before waiting in their hotel rooms until late that night. Sam wasn't sure it was necessary to arrive at Clarissa's after midnight, and he was a little bemused when he saw Macleod there, who took him up into the attic.

He was even more confused, seeing a youngish woman with black hair, dressed in black jeans and a black shirt under a leather jacket in one corner. There was another dark-haired woman who spoke with a Northern Irish accent. He saw Patterson, who he recognised from photographs, though he'd never met him. And Clarissa was sitting there, in the middle.

'I've got the photographs you asked for,' said Sam. 'The auction's all organised. We'll be back there for more photographs tomorrow, and then the auction's the day after. It's all gone well. Erin said there was quite a lot of interest. She said the auction's quite good. A bit more added than she suspected.'

'Very good,' said Clarissa. 'Photographs. Get them up on the screen for us, will you?'

Sam stood, wondering why all these people were looking at

CHAPTER 20

the photographs. The Northern Irish woman paused Clarissa from cycling through them.

'That one,' she said, 'he's familiar.' She placed a phone call, talking to someone about coming in, and Sam felt like he was a loose end.

Beside him, Erin was looking at him questioningly, but Macleod kept smiling over at them. It was approximately twenty minutes later when they could hear someone coming up the ladder into the loft. It was getting crowded now, and everyone except Macleod and Clarissa were told to sit down. The figure who approached via the ladder was wearing a jumper with a large troll-like figure on the front.

He gave a glance around at everyone there, clearly surprised at the number of people, and then turned to the Northern Irish woman and said, 'You called?'

'Emmett,' said Clarissa. 'Emmett, this is DS Sam Lemon and DC Erin Light, my two new colleagues in Glasgow on the arts team. Sam, Erin, this is DI Emmett Grump. Runs the cold case unit up in Inverness. Worked with me formerly on the arts cases as well.'

'Could have met at the station,' said Emmett.

'You're not here to meet them,' said Macleod. 'On the screen there. Who's that? Sabine says that face is familiar.'

'Sabine?' asked Sam.

'Oh,' said Clarissa. 'This is DS Sabine Ferguson. Works with Emmett but used to work for me. I'll do you a class photo book at some point.'

Emmett walked over and stared at the image on the computer screen. Then he turned back to Macleod. 'It's not the best photograph.'

'I'm afraid it was done from a secluded camera,' said Sam.

'Difficult to know exactly where you are.'

'Done pretty well,' said Kirsten.

Sam looked over at her, unaware of who she was.

'That is Kirsten,' Macleod said to Sam. 'Kirsten is an advisor.'

Macleod was giving the look that further questions were not to be asked before he then turned back to Emmett. 'Who is it?' asked Macleod.

'It's Isabelle Isbister's husband, the new one,' said Emmett.

'It is, isn't it?' said Sabine. She looked round at Macleod.

'Yes, that's what I thought,' said Macleod. 'Saw him briefly. So very briefly, at the end of that investigation. You need to find them. They'll be to do with the knife,' said Macleod. He looked over at Kirsten. 'Need them tailed to know what they're doing.'

Kirsten nodded. 'I'll get on to looking up hotels and that. They may not have come up particularly secretively. Maybe just a name change.'

Kirsten disappeared, and Macleod thanked Sam and Erin, saying they'd done a sterling job and to keep going with it. They were to do the same thing the next day.

Sam gave him a nod, but on the way back to their hotel room, he asked Erin, 'What do you make of all this?'

'I think we're not meant to make any more of it than what we're told,' said Erin, 'but I think there's a lot going on.'

'Yes,' said Sam, 'I think you're right.'

* * *

The second day of the auction viewing passed, and Isabelle Isbister's husband had turned up again. He'd picked up the knife and given it a good going over. Sam had seen him, as

CHAPTER 20

had Erin, but neither of them had spotted the blonde-haired woman in the flowery dress that had watched the man the entire way round. They didn't see her leave when he left.

After that, Kirsten had changed and tailed him all the way back to a hotel at Inverness. She sat and watched him that night, having dinner with Isabelle Isbister. She took express note of how the man seemed to quieten the woman harshly whenever she felt uncomfortable, how at times he snapped at her, telling her what to do.

When they'd gone for a walk, and then out to a bar, Kirsten noticed she said little. She was the last to bring up a conversation, the last to put anything forward of her own, instead responding to his commands, and being silent when told to. The controlling nature was obvious.

Kirsten wondered if it was always like this, or were they just away from where they lived? They were from Pitlochry, after all.

Kirsten had known love in her life, she'd known loss, and she'd known terror and pain. Over her brief life, for she wasn't even in her thirties yet, she had built up an understanding of how people reacted in certain situations. It was important, working in the Service, where you had to read people, often from a distance, to understand what was happening.

She could read Isabelle Isbister and her husband. The man dominated; the man controlled. Here was a woman who was not living a free life.

Kirsten watched as they returned to the hotel room. She was outside the door when she heard the slap, and three hours later, she was outside the door again, to hear a man snore, and a woman crying in the dark.

Isabelle had been the wife of Gavin Isbister, Macleod's

colleague. Somebody had put him in a grave, somebody had killed him, and then his wife had remarried, and come to live in Pitlochry where Gavin had died.

Kirsten didn't have any evidence to say that this was a sham marriage, that this was someone controlling the aftermath of Isbister's killing. But deep down in her gut, that's exactly what she thought.

Chapter 21

Sam Lemon was feeling a little discombobulated. All his life he'd been smart, he'd looked good, but today he was wearing a wig of rather messy hair. He'd also donned a rather scruffy beard.

He was going to an auction house with his secretary, who was, in fact, his colleague, DC Erin Light. Erin was dressed in a suit and distinctly did not look herself. Her hair was tied up into a long braid down her back, and she had a handbag that looked like it had been bought at a fashion house. Usually, Erin's handbags looked like they could carry the world.

The two of them were possibly out of their depth, certainly out of their comfort zones, but part of Sam was also excited. He had done little undercover work in his time, and all he had to do today was to bid at an auction. Sam didn't go to auctions and bid, although he was going to have to see more and more of them to understand the world he was now moving in. He was a good detective. Sam was also fit, and now having met Patterson, he realised he would be the muscle within the arts group. Something was up—something he wasn't being told everything about. And so, all Erin and he could do was get on with it. Erin made an effort and was ready on time as they went down to breakfast.

She devoured several croissants and pain au chocolat, had the orange juice and the full breakfast, while Sam had got through some porridge with added fruit. He'd indulged in a banana on the way out as well, just to keep himself going. As they drove up to the auction, he noticed Erin seemed to be quite excited.

'You will tell me if I'm doing something out of line, won't you?' he said to her.

'Of course,' said Erin.

'We've not been working together long and I think we're very much on the outside of this,' said Sam. 'So I think we do our jobs and keep our heads down and see what comes about afterwards. We have our role today, so that's what we'll do.'

'Of course,' said Erin.

'Are you okay?' asked Sam.

'I'm fine,' said Erin. 'I'm doing a job I love. I'm working in the arts field, we're on the case at the moment, and we're going to an auction. What's not to like?'

'Sorry,' said Sam. 'I'm afraid I'm a bit out of my patch at the moment, into somebody else's. It just feels like a foreign country I'm working in.'

'It'll be fine,' said Erin.

He looked at her. She really had that happy-go-lucky feeling about her.

They pulled up at the auction house, moseyed in and sat down, as did the rest of the bidders. The pair sat more towards the back, Erin saying that was the best position to see other people. Sam said they could stand at the back, but Erin said they didn't want to be too noticeable.

They'd registered and had a paddle with their specific

CHAPTER 21

number on it. They would hold up when they wanted to bid. Together, the two of them sat down and awaited the Icelandic items to come up for bidding. It was a good forty minutes before the first was presented—a small, crudely insignificant figure. Sam looked over and he spotted the husband of Isabelle Isbister.

There was some bidding online and then a couple of people within the room bid. But the man Sam was watching ever so closely didn't. Erin said Sam should put up a bid every now and again just to show that he was interested in other things and indeed in the Icelandic collection, because that would then bolster his being interested in the knife when it came up.

Six of the other items went through that Sam and Erin had put forward. Each sold for around the price they expected. And on each occasion Isabelle Isbister and her husband beside her did not bid on anything. It was then the time for the knife to be put up for bidding.

'I think there's been a bit of interest online,' said Erin. She was looking down at her phone on some sort of app that was helping her to identify what was happening.

'What's that?' said Sam.

'It's what the online bidders see. It updates at the same time.'

'What are you expecting this knife to get?' said Sam.

'A couple of thousand at most. I mean, it's interesting, but it's not, well, it's not the be-all and end-all.'

The auctioneer announced the knife, describing it as having a loose connection to Forseti. He detailed the embellishments on the handle and then began the bidding. Five hundred pounds had been bid online and instantly Isabelle Isbister's husband put up his paddle. Sam went to put his up but Erin stopped him.

'Don't do it yet. You won't look serious yet. You'll be the one hanging back, waiting to see if a fight's going on. There's plenty of time. I'll tell you what to do.'

Sam nodded and tried to appear as if he knew what was happening. He looked around the room with sharp eyes, to give the impression that he was on top of this.

The bidding rose, and soon they were through the one thousand pounds mark, shortly after one thousand, and then it died off.

'There's nothing coming through online. It's going to go once. It's going to go twice, and then you jump in, okay?'

Sam nodded. As the auctioneer said, 'Going once, going twice,' he felt his arm being lifted and the paddle being raised to the sky. 'Two thousand pounds in the corner.'

He saw Isbister's husband turn round, watching. Isbister's paddle went up again. Two thousand one hundred, two thousand two hundred, two thousand three hundred; it went back and forth.

'He's still going.'

'He is,' said Erin. 'Let's see how much he wants it.'

'He's meant to win it,' said Sam. 'We're meant to let him win it.'

'Say five. Put your paddle up and say five.'

'In the corner,' said the auctioneer, 'currently at two thousand eight hundred.'

Sam put his paddle up. 'Five thousand,' he said, trying to sound nonchalant. There was a murmur amongst the auction crowd. Nothing so far had gone for five thousand pounds.

Isbister's husband lifted himself out of the chair slightly and turned to look over. He turned back to see the auctioneer looking at him expectantly.

CHAPTER 21

'Six,' said the man.

'Go eight,' said Erin.

'Eight?' said Sam. 'Are you crazy?'

'Go eight. He's buying it.'

Sam raised his paddle. 'Eight thousand.'

The cry of 'Ten thousand!' came within two seconds.

'Blimey,' said Sam. 'He's paid five times the odds.'

'Go fifteen,' said Erin.

Sam could feel himself shaking. He was forty years of age and had seen things in combat that were so unpleasant, so vile, that it shook him to his core. Yet here he was, simply in a bidding war, and he was shaking.

'Fifteen thousand,' he said, flourishing the paddle.

'Easy,' said Erin. 'You're meant to look like you actually do this all the time.'

Sam gave a faint nod.

'Twenty thousand!' came the cry. The auctioneer looked back over towards Sam. He went to respond but Erin put her hand out.

'He's meant to buy it. You go much further, and we will make this a news item. At the moment, it's excitable. You drive this into the thirty, forty, fifty thousands and it becomes a news item. We don't want it to be a news item.'

Sam tilted his head, making it look like he was being thoughtful. And then he shook it.

That was enough. The auctioneer banged down his gavel. 'Sold!'

* * *

The auction had ended and those who had purchased were

making their way to secure their items and hand over the money. There were various people from the auction house milling about, one of whom was dressed in a smart waistcoat and trousers, the uniform of the auction house. Thankfully, several of the staff left uniform within their lockers, and Kirsten Stewart had found some that fitted her.

The key thing was staying out of sight in the main. But she was now lingering about in the room where people were paying for their items. She watched as Isabelle and her husband approached the table. There was a brief conversation, and then he produced a credit card. He used the credit card, signed some documentation, and was about to disappear.

Kirsten timed her walk to perfection, passing by and glancing down at the detail that had been signed. Tom Levant. *Who was Tom Levant?* Kirsten left the room, grabbed a large coat, put it on, and came back into the room to see Isabelle and her husband disappear.

They got into a car, and Kirsten got into her own and followed them. She expected them to return to the hotel, but they drove up north. Kirsten followed as they wound up the A9. The man stopped around Lairg, got out of the car, and looked around. He then placed a call. Kirsten had pulled off a little past him and was out of the car to check what he was doing. All the time, Isabelle Isbister simply sat there. She tried to speak only twice and each time he cut her dead with a comment.

Shortly, he returned to his car and drove back, Kirsten following him. They stopped off briefly at a restaurant, and Kirsten got herself a meal, watching the couple from a distance. Once again, Isabelle said so very little. Kirsten stared at the woman.

CHAPTER 21

Her skin looked taut from years of worry. Her black glasses, large and round, had sunken eyes behind them. The woman's hair was white, almost crinkly, but it was quite neat and short.

She was well-dressed today, having been out to the auction house. However, she ate at the speed he ate at. She finished her drink when he finished his. Everything she was doing was governed by him. *If someone was locked up in a cell, they couldn't look more like a prisoner*, Kirsten thought.

When they'd finished their meal, Kirsten followed them as they returned to the hotel. She wandered along the corridor to their room, passing by it in both directions, listening for a conversation. They eventually spoke loud enough for her to hear. There wasn't much said, except for: 'A few more days? I can't wait a few days.' And there was a slap. *Back of the hand*, Kirsten thought, *across the face*. 'You'll wait when you're told.' And then there was no more.

Kirsten kept her watch, and in the night, she heard tears. She eventually returned to the car, lying down in the car outside the hotel. She doubted they would come out until morning, but she'd be awake by five, ready for them to make a move.

The knife was still with them. Where would it go? Who would he talk to?

Kirsten knew that everything they'd done so far had led to this one contact. Who the knife got handed on to could very well give them more information. It could be the next thread to be pulled, the next group of people to be brought out into the light. There was almost excitement running through her veins, but it would be dawn at the earliest when it all kicked off. For now, she had to make her bed in the car and lie in it.

Chapter 22

Clarissa sat in a car with Kirsten, watching the hotel of Tom Levant and Isabelle Isbister. She was calling him Tom Levant because she didn't know what else to call him. He was her husband, but he was also something else.

Patterson was sitting in another car, not far away, for Kirsten advised that to tail the pair would be easier with two cars. Also, if at any point they needed to check something out, they didn't have to lose their prey. It was around about eight o'clock in the morning when Clarissa saw Levant come out. He was on his own. Isabelle was presumably still back in the hotel room.

'Shall we leave Pats here?' asked Clarissa. 'Keep an eye on Isabelle?'

'No, we both go,' said Kirsten. 'This could be a drop; in which case we might want to have a look at wherever he drops something. At some point, somebody's going to come for the knife. They might not swap it in the hotel. They might drop it somewhere quite remote. Fewer eyes to see.'

'OK,' said Clarissa. 'You do this. I'll follow your advice.'

Clarissa still hadn't got used to Kirsten. It was a different world they were operating in, one that has nearly cost Clarissa

CHAPTER 22

her life. Kirsten had been forceful, brutal in getting them out from Heligoland. And Clarissa was grateful. But Clarissa was also the boss, and she was still finding it difficult to be undercut.

The thing was that Patterson did it at times. But he did it by jibing her. He pointed out that she was wrong in an almost a humorous way, so that she would yield and follow his request. There was no fun in what Kirsten did. Everything was cold. Brutal. Maybe that was the business she was in.

Clarissa drove the car because she insisted she always did that better than Kirsten, and the woman wasn't taking everything away from her. Patterson followed, and he tailed the van north from Inverness and up the A9, before cutting off towards Altnaharra. He pulled in as he approached the stone bridge at Altnaharra. There was a river running underneath it and almost a flat boggy plain around it, brown and yellow rolling in with the occasional green. If the heather had been out, it might even have turned into a purple.

The river was wide enough and seemed to meander away from the bridge. It was oozing, and Clarissa pulled up some distance from the bridge, where Kirsten took out her binoculars. Patterson continued on past and would turn around in about two miles to come back the other way.

'What's he up to?' asked Clarissa.

'He's taken out a small package,' said Kirsten. 'I think he's putting it under the bridge.'

'Really? We just have to watch the bridge then. Then we'll get the next one up.'

'I don't like it,' said Kirsten.

'Why?' asked Clarissa.

'Look how open it is. That's a drop you're doing. A drop

shouldn't be done like this.

They'd have to get out of the car and go underneath the bridge. Why would you stop at this bridge? You might get the odd tourist stop, get out, take a photograph. But otherwise, you will not stop here.'

'Somebody might go down fishing in the river,' suggested Clarissa. 'That would be a good cover. Pop under the bridge, pick it up. Put it in your fishing bag, away you go again.'

Kirsten glanced over at her. 'You sure you haven't done this kind of stuff before?'

That almost sounded like a compliment, thought Clarissa. *Maybe she's warming to me.*

'Levant's leaving,' said Kirsten.

'Well then, we're going to need to stay and watch,' said Clarissa, messaging on her phone. 'I'll tell Pats to follow him. See where he goes.'

The man pulled off in the car and Clarissa soon saw Patterson crossing the bridge, tailing Levant back toward Inverness.

'We can't sit here in a car all day watching this,' said Kirsten. 'Certainly not if somebody's going to get close. We're going to need to hide the car.'

'Well, we could get Pats standing nearby, couldn't we?' said Clarissa.

'No, if we're going to get closer, we have to get out there. Out into the moor.' Kirsten retreated into the boot and pulled out an item. 'You're going to like this,' said Kirsten.

'Why don't I just stay near the car?'

'No, I think you should watch closely.'

'Why?' asked Clarissa.

'So we can identify, or at least, get a description of who makes the grab, in case we lose them after. That means you're

CHAPTER 22

going to be in a position where you need to stay prone and you will not want to be spotted. But that's a position I can't act from if I need to intervene. It would be difficult. It's better if I use the car. We've got to think of your protection, though.'

'So what have you got for me?' asked Clarissa.

'It's like a shawl,' said Kirsten. 'You wrap it round you and you lie down in the grass. And make sure you keep a beanie on for that head of yours until your hair grows back.'

It didn't take long before Kirsten had wrapped a shawl-come-camouflage blanket around Clarissa and placed a camouflaged beanie hat on her head.

She indicated to Clarissa how to get to a suitable hiding point. And twenty minutes later, Clarissa was sitting there, watching the bridge. She was down low in the grass and thought it would be hard to spot her. The difficult bit was that she was going to have to remain calm. The good side was few cars came past here, so she could stretch in between their passing by.

Clarissa spent the day out on the boggy moor with visits from Kirsten, who brought her food and drinks. By the time night had fallen, Clarissa was getting fed up. She checked her watch; it was three in the morning and her eyes were drooping. At three, there really wasn't any traffic and Clarissa was shaking herself back and forward trying to keep out the cold. It was then she heard the distant sound of a car.

She froze, and kept her binoculars trained on the bridge. Kirsten said she would watch the car approach, get a number plate if she had to, but Clarissa should keep the focus on the bridge. Clarissa had a microphone and a little earpiece so she could keep contact with Kirsten.

'Someone's coming,' she said.

'Slowing down,' said Kirsten. 'Keep your eyes on them.'

A stately car pulled up, and a chauffeur climbed out. He opened the rear door and a man in a suit, who was difficult to see, emerged and stood on the bridge. He looked around for a moment and then gave a nod to the chauffeur. Kirsten watched as the chauffeur went over the edge.

'I can't see them very well,' said Clarissa.

'It's okay,' said Kirsten. 'I can follow them.'

'Did you get a number plate?'

'Yes,' said Kirsten. 'I've messaged it, but it's a false one.'

'How do you know that quick?'

'I have my means and my friends. If I say it's false, it's false. Not that it's surprising.'

'Can you get a good idea of who the man is?' asked Clarissa.

'Not from this distance. It is very dark.'

'Maybe if I got closer,' said Clarissa. 'I could get a look at his face. I mean, they will not see me moving at this time of night, will they? It's so dark out here, and with this camo on.'

'I don't like it,' said Kirsten. 'At the moment, they don't know we're here. It's going to be hard enough to tail them. After all, how many cars have you seen in the last hour?'

'Other than this one, none.'

'Exactly, so they're driving out on silent roads. That makes them think, "Somebody's behind me, it's three in the morning. What are they doing here?"'

'You said before that you weren't happy with the place. Do you think this is a trap?' asked Clarissa.

'I don't know. Seems strange to have turned up in a car like this, with a chauffeur.

You feel this might be somebody who's quite important?'

'That's what I'm thinking,' said Clarissa. 'I'm thinking this is for real. We need to get up close. We need to find out who this is.'

'Hold your horses,' said Kirsten. 'You don't know if this is real or not. Got to err on the side of caution.'

'If they get out of here and we haven't been able to tail them, we have nothing,' said Clarissa. 'If I get up and I get an ID, or I get an image of them, well then, we've got something to go on.'

'You get too close,' said Kirsten, 'and they spot you, then you're in trouble. You're in the middle of a moor.'

'It's worth the risk,' said Clarissa.

'I don't think that's a sound judgment call.'

'Well, I'm the boss,' said Clarissa, 'so it's what I'm doing.'

To her credit, Kirsten said nothing, and Clarissa crawled forward. It was hard going, but the people on the bridge seemed to take a long time. Clarissa was close to the river and kept following it closer and closer to the bridge. There was no moonlight. No sudden beam to light up the man on the bridge. He had his back to her, but his suit looked smart.

'You don't want to go closer than that,' said Kirsten.

'I can get closer,' whispered Clarissa. 'They haven't seen me. I need to get up towards the bridge. Look, I can see the chauffeur now. I think he's under the bridge.'

Clarissa saw the chauffeur scrabbling about, the man on the bridge looking away from her, and decided she could move much quicker if she didn't crawl. She stood up slightly, but the camouflaged shawl hung off her.

Surely that will be okay in the dark. I can drop back down if I needed.

As she stole forward, she could feel the cold through her knees. Why on earth am I doing this? This is a young woman's game. And then she berated herself. I'm the Rottweiler. The moment you think about being too old for something, you become it!

She quickened up her pace.

'Get down,' said Kirsten.

Clarissa dropped onto the grass. 'What did you see?' asked Clarissa.

'Nothing,' said Kirsten. 'But you are getting too close.'

'If I don't get any closer, I won't be able to see them. I might only get one chance when he turns around.'

'Don't get too close. The closer you are, the easier it is to shoot you. The further away, the harder.'

'What can you see from your bit?'

'I'm not at my bit,' said Kirsten.

'Where are you then?' asked Clarissa.

'I'm on the move. Don't worry. Just stay where you are.'

The hell with this? thought Clarissa. *I need to get close. I won't see him at this distance.*

She looked up at the man's suit. He was on the bridge, so there was the height, and at the moment she could just barely see the top of his bottom and the neat cut of the suit rising to the shoulders. His hair was indistinct.

She wasn't close enough to pick it out as sections, just one mass of colour. So, if she didn't get closer, she wouldn't see the face when he turned. Clarissa got up onto her knees again, then into a crouch. She crept forward. Her knees may not have been cracking loudly, but she felt like they were. She felt like they were being forced into actions they never should. The shawl hung heavy on her back. And she could still feel the bruising from Heligoland.

Clarissa remembered the man smashing her back into the wall. She remembered pulling the knife on him. For a moment

CHAPTER 22

she froze, the memory all she could feel, and then she crept forward once more.

It was working. She was now getting up close to the bridge. She could only be what, thirty yards away? Or maybe fifty? For a moment, she thought about what club she would take out. What would it take to land a golf ball on the bridge? That was the way Clarissa's mind worked with distances. What club would you take? This one wouldn't even be a quarter-hit wedge, would it?

And then she froze. Clarissa looked over to the right-hand side by the bridge. She thought she could see a shadow. Did it move? Did that shadow actually flinch? She hunkered down again and stared ever so intently into the gloom. Crouching as she walked ever so slowly, she made towards the shadow, and then she stopped. The shadow moved, and she thought she could see the barrel of a gun pointing directly at her.

Chapter 23

Clarissa froze, seeing the barrel point towards her. She couldn't see the figure behind it, not clearly, but she knew they were going to shoot. She knew she was in trouble, big trouble, possibly terminal trouble. Maybe she should have jumped out of the way, she should have hit the ground, but nothing sparked within her—only a dread, almost a resignation.

Something hit her, like she'd been hit by a bus, only it didn't come from in front. It wasn't a bullet impacting her chest. It was somebody knocking the living daylights out of her, sending her flying.

Clarissa's left shoulder hit the ground hard, and she rolled for a moment. Whoever had hit her was rolling, too. She thought she heard a quiet shot, like a silenced weapon.

'Stay down,' said an angry voice. Clarissa lay flat, but she scanned around her as best she could.

Kirsten had hit her, and hit her hard, but she'd probably saved her life. She couldn't find the woman, though. She was gone. Clarissa didn't like being in this prone position. When should she move? She looked back in the direction that the shot had come from, but the person who had delivered it was on the move, running upright and heading up to the top of the bridge. The man in the suit was climbing inside the car, too.

'Get to the car, quick as you can,' said Kirsten. 'Our car!'

Clarissa stood up and wondered how wise that was, but she had an instruction. In fact, it was delivered like an order.

She felt her shoulder aching, her feet cold, but Clarissa marched over towards the road. Kirsten had left the car some distance further up but Clarissa was moving as quick as she could.

The men had got into the other car. Kirsten had told her to move, and Clarissa just assumed it was perfectly okay to do so. She wouldn't know any different. She couldn't see anyone. But she started running. Well, it was more of a jog. Clarissa didn't really run.

She got to the car, threw off the camouflage shawl into the back seat. The keys were in the car. Clarissa jumped into the driver's seat, and started the engine. She dropped the handbrake, put the car into gear and went to drive off, there was an almighty banging on the back windscreen. Clarissa halted, and the passenger door opened. Kirsten jumped in.

'Thanks for—'

'Get after them,' said Kirsten. 'You said you can drive—do it.'

The woman sounded angry, but Clarissa did as instructed. The car ahead was already well clear of the bridge, but with no one else here, it was easier to spot them.

In the dark of the night, the brightness of the headlights made the other car stand out, and Clarissa tore after them.

Kirsten reached across, and Clarissa found her headlights being switched off. 'They don't want to know where we are. They don't want to know how close we are. If we're lucky, they might even slow down, assuming we're not following them.'

'But I can't see particularly well.'

'No, but we'll catch them quicker this way. Trust me. You said you can drive. Drive!'

It had been a full day out there in the moor, and suddenly Clarissa was having to go from zero to a hundred and twenty. She was, however, in her element.

She always felt she could drive better than anyone else, especially on the team. And right now, she was showing it. The pedal was down on the floor, and she was taking corners like a rally driver gone berserk. Cutting across the road, swinging in at the right time, judging them to perfection and powering out of them. It only took her a mile to be close up on the other car.

The car didn't handle quite as well as her own little green beast. But on the bright side, it wasn't her own. And she was being much less risk averse than she would be with her little green number. She loved that car. This . . . well, this was somebody else's.

She saw her quarry up ahead, and despite having the lights off, she continued at full pelt. Her foot was on and off the brake to take the corners as hard as she could. Occasionally, she dropped her hand onto the handbrake as well.

Spinning the wheel. Taking corners like a rally driver. Her car sliding rather than steering round corners. And then she saw it. The opportunity she'd been desperate for.

There was a tough bend coming up and Clarissa could just about see it in the distance. It was where a farm path came out to the road and the bend almost went at right angles off to the left.

The car in front slowed, and Clarissa saw her opportunity. As the other car began to turn the corner, she didn't slow

CHAPTER 23

down. It did and Clarissa's car caught the side of it knocking it through the open hedgerow straight into the path of the farm. She had, of course, her seatbelt on and hit it hard enough that the airbag deployed. This was a good job because Kirsten hadn't put her seatbelt on, and she hit the airbag hard.

For a moment, everything seemed to go quiet. Clarissa looked up, her heart beating fast, and she was shaking. Her back was in agony as the bruises that she'd taken before got a repeat dose.

She'd been bounced and jostled as she'd hit the other car, but she saw it suddenly spurt back into life, to drive up the farm track. It wasn't in the best of condition, though, spluttering. Clarissa reached down and started her own car, pulling the deflated air bag out of the way.

Thankfully, the engine took. Kirsten, beside her, looked somewhat bewildered, and Clarissa didn't wait for instruction. Instead, she drove after the other car.

It stopped at a large barn, with no road to go anywhere else, and Clarissa piled into the back of it. This time, Kirsten was flung forward onto no protection. Fortunately, the speed wasn't as great, maybe only twenty miles an hour or so, but Kirsten hit the passenger dashboard of the car hard, and then fell back into her seat. Clarissa still had her seatbelt on.

'Are you okay?' Clarissa asked Kirsten. She saw the woman shake her head momentarily, stare out of the window, and then the car door was open with no response forthcoming. Clarissa watched as Kirsten ran forward. The chauffeur and his passenger were out of the car, and Kirsten was sprinting full tilt before leaping at them, and bringing down the passenger.

Clarissa opened the car door and stumbled out. She saw the chauffeur pull something out of a jacket pocket, which looked like a nightstick or something. He hit Kirsten in the back as she was holding his passenger. She cried out, and Clarissa ran forward.

Remembering those glorious rugby days of her youth, she dipped her shoulder, hitting the chauffeur square on the hip. It took him down to the ground in what she thought was one of the best tackles of her life. Her body disagreed though, screaming at her, but the adrenaline was pumping. She felt around with her hand and grabbed hold of the driver's ear, pulling it hard and hearing him yell. Clarissa pummelled a fist down onto his head. After all, they'd shot at her. She would not make the mistake that you simply tried to arrest these people. This was a fight you had to win. If you were subduing them, you had to knock them out. She didn't have a weapon after all. There was no gun to keep them silent. And there was no knife in her pocket either.

Clarissa was hit by the chauffeur from his position on the ground, but because of the angle and their closeness, the punch wasn't strong. Clarissa hung on, twisting his ear, wondering if she'd end up ripping it off. But in the back of her mind, something was bothering her.

There'd been three people out there, one who had taken a shot at her. Where was he? She was now kneeling on top of the chauffeur. Clarissa was fighting, holding down his fists, willing to get another punch away. But the barn door opened. As she looked up towards it, a man stepped out. He held a shotgun in his hand. He wasn't pointing at Clarissa, though. Instead, he was pointing at Kirsten.

Just as the shotgun roared, Clarissa saw Kirsten spinning over, holding the man she'd attacked in front of her. A second shot thundered. There was a moment when blood spurted

CHAPTER 23

and then Kirsten seemed to almost casually dump the man in the suit to one side.

The shotgun was being snapped open, one cartridge was replaced. Kirsten jumped up onto her feet. A hand went down, hauling Clarissa to her feet, before Kirsten charged at the man with the gun. He fumbled quickly with the second cartridge, trying to load again, but she hit him quicker than that. The shotgun was knocked out of the way and Kirsten drove the man backwards. He went down with a punch, as Kirsten shouted back at Clarissa to get into the car. Clarissa turned away and Kirsten continued to rain punches down, the man's face becoming bloody.

Clarissa, however, had run for the car and jumped in. She turned the engine over—it took two tries, but it started. She began to reverse, pulling it away from the other car. And then she saw Kirsten struggling to get back up to her feet. The woman must have been exhausted. But she also saw the chauffeur now recovering from her administrations and reaching down for the shotgun that had fallen.

Kirsten was a distance from it and the chauffeur picked it up and, as he snapped the barrels back into place, Kirsten turned and saw him. He lifted it up, almost gleefully pointing it at her.

Clarissa wasn't fast on her feet. Clarissa was not an all-action person and every part of her was hurting now. But one area in which she excelled was in handling a car. As soon as she saw the man get up with the gun and snap the barrels into place, the car was rolling. As he went to fire, Clarissa drove into the side of him, knocking the man flying, the gun falling from his hands.

Clarissa watched him roll onto the bonnet and then fall down the other side. Kirsten ran over to the car and jumped into the passenger's seat.

'Go! We go!'

'What do you mean, "We go?" We've got these guys. We have—'

'This isn't it,' said Kirsten. 'The man in the suit. They shot at the man in the suit. This is a decoy. You don't shoot your boss like that.'

Clarissa couldn't quite work out what was going on, but she knew how to reverse a car out of the track and onto the road. As she did so, Kirsten was picking up her phone.

'Who are you on to?'

'Pats. He needs to get them.'

'Who?' asked Clarissa.

'Isabelle Isbister and Levant. They've been compromised. This was all a setup to see if they were being tracked. Pats needs to get them, to warn them. They'll have been watched. They'll be at the place for the proper meet. This lot knows they're there. This has gone wrong. They'll be told. They'll go for them.'

Kirsten held the phone to her ear as Clarissa tore off back down the road, heading towards Inverness. As she rounded one corner, Kirsten almost nonchalantly said to her, 'You can put the lights on now.' Clarissa flicked them on. There was only one working.

'Get whatever you can from this baby,' said Kirsten, tapping the passenger side dash of the car. 'If they get rid of them, we really will have nothing.'

Chapter 24

Eric Patterson sat in the car, watching the small cottage at Bonar Bridge, north of Inverness. Having returned from his trip to Altnaharra, he had tailed Levant back to his Inverness hotel, where he had picked up Isabelle. They'd made for the cottage in Bonar Bridge that evening.

It had been quiet watching them. They didn't seem to do anything. They'd gone inside the cottage and hadn't come out. At first, Patterson was worried he'd missed them, but he'd walked past and glimpsed them inside. The others had been waiting for the pick-up up at Altnaharra, and nothing had happened. And so now, at about half three in the morning, Patterson was feeling sleepy.

He was wondering how it was all going to work. After all, he was here on his own, keeping a watch. The other two were up there. Clarissa and Kirsten could take it in turns. One could sleep while the other watched.

He had nobody with him. Maybe they should have called someone else to come out. Perry, maybe. Perry always seemed to be a good person to be with. He always thought about you, as far as Patterson could see.

Clarissa didn't always work like that. And then Patterson

stopped himself. The woman had saved his life, after all. Although she maybe could have taken a little blame for how close they'd got to those that had slit his throat. One thing that was bothering Patterson was the levels they were going to with all this. He joined the arts division for a calmer life, after having had his neck slashed.

Then, he'd been down in London and seen someone have their head blown off in front of him. He'd disappeared out of the country, fought people in tunnels underground, before having to act for his life on the way back out. Now, he was watching a couple who were part, it was believed, of a much bigger organisation which was operating within the UK—killing people who they determined not to be fit.

Or at least, so the story went. It wasn't exactly what he'd imagined when moving to the arts team.

He could feel his phone vibrating and so Patterson picked it up and saw it was Kirsten. He pressed the button and lazily put the phone to his ear.

'Where are you?' asked Kirsten.

'Bonar Bridge. They're still inside.'

'Get them out. They have to leave.'

'What?' said Patterson.

'Listen. They have to leave. This has all been a setup. They're in danger. Go there. Knock on the door. Just tell them they have to go. It's a setup. Get them out! Someone will come to kill them. You won't be able to hold those sorts of people off, Patterson. You need to get to them before the despatch squad gets there. Get Levant and Isabelle out of there. Take them to Macleod. He can find the Service. The Service can hide them. Get them to Macleod. We're on our way.'

'What do you mean, you're on your way?'

CHAPTER 24

'I'll tell you when we get there. Do what I ask. Right now!'

'What am I meant to say to him?' asked Patterson.

'I don't know, but you've got to convince them. You're the only thing standing between them and a bullet.' The phone went dead.

Patterson's heart pounded. This certainly wasn't something he was expecting. Sometimes, though, the body works on automatic, and Patterson was getting out of the car before he'd even thought about formulating a plan. As he walked over to the short driveway of the cottage and then up to the front door, he still wasn't sure what he was going to do.

There was a doorbell, and so he rang it. Much to his surprise, however, the door was opened quickly, and Tom Levant stood there fully dressed. 'Who the hell are you?'

Patterson reached inside his jacket and pulled out his warrant card. 'DC Eric Patterson. I know what you've been up to. I know about the package you put up at Altnaharra. However, I have been reliably informed by a colleague that it's a setup. I tailed you back from there, back to your hotel in Inverness and out to here. They will come for you—the ones you are working with.'

Patterson saw a gun being produced by Levant and pointed at him.

'What the hell are you on?' asked Levant.

'You don't have the time. My colleagues have been attacked up there. It's gone wrong. They're coming for the knife and they're coming for you. You have been compromised.'

'And you have compromised me,' said Levant.

The gun was waved, showing that Patterson should enter the house, and then the living room. He did so and was told to sit down. Isabelle Isbister entered the room, looking drawn.

It was half three in the morning, so everyone was tired, but the circumstances seemed to play on her much more than Levant. Although his eyes seemed to get wilder by the second.

Levant picked up a mobile phone as Isabelle spoke to him. 'What's wrong? What's happening?'

'The false package he asked me to leave, up by Altnaharra. Been tailed. They know. They'll come for us.'

'What do you mean they come for us?' said Isabelle. 'I've done everything. Ever since they killed Gavin, I haven't stepped out of line.'

'They don't care about that,' said Levant. He held the phone up to his ear. There was a silence in the room. Then he shook his head. 'No answer.'

'What does that mean?' said Isabelle.

'It means our friend here is correct,' said Levant. 'It means they're going to come for us. I wondered. They told me it was a decoy run. Told me to put the dummy one up there. And you don't refuse them, not when they ask. They've been on to us. His lot.'

Isabelle sat down suddenly, shaking.

'You can go, though,' said Patterson. 'We can get you into cover.'

'Police cover will not work,' said Levant.

'It's not just the police that's working on this. We have people. People who work in the agencies. We can get you underground, get you out of here. You'll not run away on your own. It'll not work.'

Levant stood up for a moment, walking round. 'Fine,' he said. 'I'll go with you. But I'll drive to go somewhere first. You with me.'

'You'll take her too,' said Patterson. 'They won't do a deal without her.'

'Yeah, they will. What is she? Just somebody that got played in all of this.'

'I'm sat right here,' said Isabelle suddenly. But the man swung the back of his hand, hitting her hard and drawing blood from her mouth.

'Just sit there and shut up.'

'You'll need me,' said Patterson. 'You don't bring her, I don't go either.'

'And what? I leave you here? You'll be dead?'

'Smart choice is to come. All of us. All of us go now and hide.' Levant wandered about for a moment.

'We have to be quick. But you're coming with me,' he said to Patterson. 'We all go. But you'll be my cover. We run into our guys early, I can give you up to them. They might let me go. You'll be my shield, copper,' said Levant.

Patterson wondered what plan he was formulating, but it didn't seem to be a definite one. One moment, he was talking about handing Patterson over to the group. Then Patterson was there to help him with the police. Then he was a shield in case people shot at him. Isabelle too. Patterson guessed there weren't many good options going through his head.

'Out to the car.'

Patterson walked at gunpoint to the car in the driveway and was told to get into the front and drive it. He was handed the keys by Levant, and Isabelle was put into the rear. The gun was placed in Patterson's ribs, and he drove away from the small cottage, turning up and then over towards the steel bridge crossing at Bonar Bridge.

As he turned onto it, there was a car coming from the other direction. Without warning, it spun and blocked the road.

Behind them, another car pulled up and spun too to block the road behind.

'Shit,' said Levant. 'They're here. You, out!' he spat at Patterson.

The night was dark and as Patterson stepped out of the car, he was sweating. His body felt icy, almost numb. He wondered what he would be facing. He was told to move away from the car and to stand on the road as someone in a suit approached. The man had a scarf across his face, and there was a chauffeur beside him.

Patterson looked behind, and there were two men by the other car, both holding guns.

'Time is up, Levant,' said the man in the suit. 'I take it you have the knife. It's up to you. If we have to take you, it won't be pleasant. Or you could do your duty by the society.'

Patterson wondered at the words. But when he looked at Levant, the man was white, trembling now. Patterson watched him reach inside his jacket pocket and he pulled out the sacrificial knife. He took it, placed it in front of him, almost like a Japanese warrior about to commit hara-kiri.

'Don't! Don't!' said Patterson. Isabel Isbister was standing at the man's side, and she screamed as he drove the sacrificial knife straight in at the height of his heart. His face twisted in pain, and he tumbled down to the ground. Patterson dived after him, turned the man over, and hauled the knife out.

Blood was pouring everywhere. Patterson put his hand on the wound, trying to stop the blood flow, but in truth, Levant looked dead. There was nothing cohesive from the man, the body spasming, and then Patterson heard laughter. He turned to see the man in the suit, his shoulders rising and falling as he laughed. Isabelle had turned away, her hand over her mouth.

CHAPTER 24

Bastards, thought Patterson, *to laugh at a man like this.* He quietly slipped the knife from Levant's hand, and carefully into his pocket.

'Oh no, no,' said the man in the suit. 'We'll be having that.' The chauffeur behind him had raised a gun, pointing it at Patterson. 'You can either bring it over and hand it to us, and we'll make your end very swift. But if I have to come and get it, well, let's say you'll have a couple of days to regret your decision. A couple of days of extreme pain, before we finally put you at your rest.'

Patterson looked behind him. The men from that car stood holding guns as well. But for a moment, Patterson thought he saw a car further away, or at least a light from it. But then it had gone out.

'What's it going to be, copper?' said the man. 'Bet you're one of Macleod's, aren't you? Yes. I wondered if he would give up. Wondered why they had picked him for the fight. It's not in his nature to stop, is it? It really isn't. But time's getting on. Bring the knife over.'

Patterson reached down into his pocket and took the knife out. For a moment, he looked at it and then gave a smile to the man in the suit before putting the knife back inside his jacket. 'Police officer. I don't comply like that,' said Patterson. 'I don't—'

He never got to finish the sentence, for behind him a car ploughed into the one which was blocking the road. Two men screamed, and the man who was pointing the gun at Patterson fired it. But it was now pointed over Patterson's shoulder, aiming at something else.

Patterson didn't hesitate. He turned and ran, grabbing Isabelle's hand. Making straight to the edge of the bridge, he jumped off, dragging Isabelle over as well. He heard shots as he fell. He didn't know if they were aimed at him. Patterson knew nothing except he was getting off that bridge.

The water was icy as he splashed into the river. But thankfully, it didn't take him back under the bridge, instead driving him further downstream and south, away from the bridge.

Breaking the surface, he gulped for air, his hand still holding on to Isabelle. He looked to see if she'd come up, but she hadn't. He grabbed hold of her, pulling her out above the surface. She was unconscious, or so he thought. Certainly, she was not showing any sign of responding. He didn't know if she was dead. But he let the river take him.

It dragged him across to the riverside and he felt the riverbed beneath his feet. Patterson pushed hard up out of the river towards the bank. There were shots up on the bridge.

As soon as he was at a depth close to knee height, Patterson picked up Isabelle and flung her over his shoulder. He may have been scrawnier than the likes of Perry, but Patterson was strong. His muscles were sinewy, and they were effective. His heart was thumping, wondering what to do next. He'd never really been in a situation like this. It sounded like there was open warfare on the bridge.

He decided he would make for the road and then maybe for a house. Call 999. Get help there. He scrambled up the bank with Isabelle on his shoulder, his feet pushing hard. He was exhausted. His legs were cold, his body shivering. But he would go on. He hadn't had his throat slit to just die like this. There was something about that horror. It almost made him feel invincible.

As he emerged off the bank and up to the roadside, a car

CHAPTER 24

pulled up. It was absolutely battered, like an old banger in a stock car race. Although the rear of the car seemed to have got off lightly. Except for the blown-out back window. The driver's window rolled down, and he saw the smiling face of a bald-headed woman. It was Clarissa. Looking up the road towards the bridge, he saw someone running down, firing a gun back towards the bridge.

'Get her in,' said Clarissa, and Patterson opened the rear door, pushing Isabelle inside. He clambered in with her, her legs on his lap, and closed the door. He glanced out the back window, through the gap where the glass had been, and saw Kirsten firing up towards the bridge. She then turned and got into the car.

'Go!' she shouted. 'Go!'

They drove off fast, Clarissa putting her foot to the floor. They were heading southeast towards the coast and passing another bridge. Kirsten told Clarissa to slow down, and she flung her gun out into the water below. Clarissa continued again.

'Towards Dornoch,' said Kirsten. 'I have a place, a safe house in Dornoch.' And she turned and looked towards Patterson. 'Is she all right?'

He stared at the prone woman on his lap. Her chest was rising and falling. 'Well, she's breathing,' he said.

The car raced on, no headlights on, until they got to Dornoch. On the outskirts of the town was a small farmhouse that looked almost derelict. The car was driven into a barn, and Patterson carried Isabel inside the farmhouse. The outer rooms were a mess of broken furniture and decay.

But underneath some floorboards was a locked door. It opened up to a small underground room, which was well equipped. There was a medical camp bed. A microwave had power and there was a small supply of tin cans. And it also had heating, which Patterson gave thanks for in his current shocked state. As Patterson sat down in a chair, he found a cup of coffee being placed in his hand by Clarissa. She was smiling at him. He couldn't get used to the bald head, though.

'Well done, Pats,' she said. 'Well done!' He stood up, put his cup down, and hugged her. 'Are you okay?' he said.

But Clarissa cried on his shoulder. She broke off for a moment, her tear-ridden eyes looking back at Patterson.

'I'm just glad you're still here,' she said, and they hugged again.

Chapter 25

'Not on your own today, then?'

Macleod sat at the picnic bench with the flask of coffee and three cups out. However, he was on his own at the bench as Anna Hunt emerged from some trees. She wore stylish black boots, black trousers, and a coat that was black as well. Her hair had clearly been brushed, and all things considered, she seemed in a good mood.

'Needed a lift,' said Macleod, and nodded over to a car sat a little way off.

'Coffee again? I must be special,' said Anna.

'Well, I like to give coffee to my friends. I am considering you a friend.'

'Well, I would hope so,' said Anna. 'Besides, I want to say thank you.'

'For?' asked Macleod.

'Isabelle Isbister. She'll be safe until this whole mess is over. She says thank you as well. I told her you were the one behind getting her out.'

'I hadn't intended that,' said Macleod. 'It was, well, something that happened.'

'No. It was your people. You have good people. There was

a mysterious suicide on the bridge at Bonar but from what I heard from my people, not everything added up.'

'Not everything added up to the ACC as well. Your people, Anna?' asked Macleod.

She shook her head. 'When things happen,' he continued, 'you often clean up. You make it not be a public thing. These people, they seem to be able to do it too.'

'We're dealing with some very high-up people,' said Anna. 'Isabelle will help.'

'It was rough,' said Macleod. 'Patterson told me it was rough. It spooked Clarissa. She's in the car.'

'I know,' said Anna. 'I'm well aware she's there.'

'Of course you do,' said Macleod, smiling. He poured the coffee, three cups, and then he turned and waved Clarissa over from the car. She was dressed in her tartan trews and shawl, but also wore a plain headscarf. As she approached, she looked suspiciously at Anna Hunt.

'Ah, the redoubtable Detective Inspector Urquhart,' said Anna. 'You've done very well.'

'I didn't think I was taking scorecards from the likes of yourself.'

'Easy,' said Macleod. 'Anna's a friend.'

'Well, you pick your friends,' Clarissa said to Macleod.

'Tell Anna what you know, or what you've found out since,' said Macleod.

'Something that I don't know?' queried Anna.

'Clarissa's speciality is the arts world,' said Macleod. 'Clarissa knows her stuff.'

'We found a dig site in Heligoland,' said Clarissa. 'The more research I've done into it and the shape of it, it seems to be about sacrifice, and around Forseti. He's a figure in the northern mythologies of Europe. I think the practice is being brought back of retribution, of making things correct. The knife was used to kill those in a circle, a way of bringing correction to the land. It seems the Frisian farmers on Heligoland may have practiced the ritual. Or some of them at least. Somebody else has tapped into that.'

'Copying them?'

'No,' said Macleod. 'This is a society. Maybe based on the old practice but with a life of its own. Patterson said that Levant, Isabelle Isbister's second husband killed himself. He stabbed himself with the knife when told to do the right thing. There was something in that. It's like a religious effort. It's not easy to kill yourself. To be afraid of what they're going to do to you so that suicide is the better option,' said Macleod. 'Forseti. And the practices around Forseti. They seem to be deeply seeped into the group's psyche.'

'I think it'll re-emerge. I think the practices are deeply tied into this group,' said Clarissa. 'God knows why. God knows why you would think like this. But they seem to. They also preserved the dig site. It should have been destroyed underneath Heligoland. But they actively set up a way to get back into it. It became something for them. It wasn't just a legend, but was somewhere they had to go back to. Somewhere they would use, I fully believe they would have met there.'

'Maybe I'll swing by, take a look,' said Anna. 'Is Kirsten about?'

'She is,' said Macleod.

'Keep her close,' said Anna. 'Knives, sacrifice. And the ability to clean up. I don't like this, Seoras,' said Anna. 'I really don't. I should know about stuff like this. People like this should be on the radar. And I'm struggling. I am really struggling.'

'Maybe they're aware of you,' said Macleod. 'Maybe they can see you coming. Maybe they're within your group.'

Anna Hunt didn't look shocked, but picked up her cup and drank some coffee. 'I think they are,' said Anna. 'Godfrey, my predecessor, worked alongside them, I'm sure of it. He wasn't part of them, but he was happy to let them function. But that was Godfrey. Godfrey was cold and callous.'

'Whereas you are as sweet as the morning dew,' said Clarissa.

'You and I, Inspector Urquhart, are very alike,' said Anna.

Clarissa raised an eyebrow. 'I'm not sure I see that.'

'You bend the rules; you do what's necessary, but you come down on the side of right,' said Anna. 'You believe in justice. I believe in protecting the country, the nations, believe in society carrying on. I believe in making sure that people are not unfairly dealt with. Sure, I may have to operate a little in the dark, but don't we all. We seek to protect the things we love, whether that be art, people, or whatever. But I work for good. I just work a little differently to my friend Seoras here.'

'And I'll let you go to work,' said Macleod. 'I'm out.'

'You're out?' said Anna, a little surprised.

'I'm out. Here,' he said.

Macleod handed over the sacrificial knife that Hope had found on the boat, the one that Levant had stabbed himself with and that Patterson had recovered. He held it forward and Anna picked it up, turning it over in her hand.

'The markings on it match some of those at the dig site. It belongs to there, or at least to somewhere similar,' said Clarissa. 'They cut across the throat with it, execution style, sacrificial.'

'As far as I'm concerned, the issue's closed to me. It's yours, Anna,' said Macleod. 'Isabelle Isbister is safe. You have her. You've promised to keep her safe until this is over. I've done what I needed to do. Gavin Isbister's name is clear. His wife is safe. Or as safe as I could ever get her. I have put all of my team under threat to do it. So, I'm out. We're stepping back. I can't put them under more risk. Not against something like this.'

He looked away, and she chuckled.

'Oh, Seoras.' Anna walked round behind him, placing a hand on his shoulder. She leant down close to his ear, but she said it loud enough for Clarissa to hear as well. 'You're fooling no one, Seoras. For the only person to fool here is me. And I ain't fooled. You will keep going. Yes, you may bide your time. You may pick your moment. But this isn't over. You're like me. You can't abide this. A society? Dealing out its own justice? Acting as if it's God? That bit must truly offend.'

Macleod didn't react, but inside, he wondered just how well she knew him. The God comment was too accurate.

'I think I've had enough,' said Clarissa. 'I lost my hair. My back is bruised as anything. I've almost been killed. I had to crash a car several times just to keep your agent alive.'

'Not my agent,' said Anna, straightening up to Clarissa. 'Kirsten's not my agent. You might be his Rottweiler. But Kirsten? Kirsten's his agent.' She turned and looked at Macleod who was shocked at the comment.

'You were the one that trained her. She trained with the Service. You taught her how to kill, taught her how to place bugs,' said Macleod. 'It was you who taught her how to infiltrate, how to get inside somewhere, who taught her how to track people.'

'That's just craft,' said Anna. 'Her ethics come from you. Her decision-making comes from you. Clarissa's doesn't come from you, but they're similar. It's what you do. You have this entire team,' said Anna, 'varied and diverse but yet, within it, they all have that core. I could be corny and say it's because they all care. But sometimes, corny's right. They do. They care about things being made right. It's why you attract them. Because that's you at the core.'

Anna drank the last of her coffee and put her cup down. 'Don't be mistaken,' she said. 'There will be a response. You can't walk away from this. You can't say "I've downed tools. Don't come after me. Don't think I'm involved anymore." You're involved. All of you.'

Clarissa looked coldly at her but Anna simply nodded.

'A response from who?' asked Macleod.

'Who? Well, this society for one. You're getting close, you're injuring them, but also the hard done by. These worshippers of Forseti on one hand and those they have injured on the other. Both are seeking something, the hard done by for this all to be highlighted, to be put right. Ironic that they're trying to put it right in a way that reminds us of Forseti's people. And Forseti's people want it all to go back to the way it was, in the dark, with no one knowing how they dispense their justice. They want control back.

'There will be a response. Be looking for it, Seoras. I'll help where I can. I will investigate. We will find who wields this,' she said, holding up the knife before the two of them. 'In the meantime, stay safe. Keep Kirsten close. They will come.'

She tucked the knife into her pocket. Anna went to walk away before she stopped and turned back.

'Thanks for the coffee. Excellent as ever.'

Macleod watched as she disappeared through the trees.

'You like her, don't you?' said Clarissa.

'She's quite a formidable woman,' said Macleod.

CHAPTER 25

'You could just have said yes,' said Clarissa. 'I'm not Jane, it's all right. If you've looked at a woman and liked her, you know, you don't have to hide it from me.'

'She's got a forcefulness, determination, like you,' said Macleod.

He drank his coffee and put the cups back in a little bag along with the flask, before indicating that Clarissa should finish hers.

'You always meet out here?' asked Clarissa.

'Usually somewhere private.'

'Well, I wouldn't tell Jane that bit. That bit sounds really dodgy.'

'Are you okay?' asked Macleod. 'I kind of asked you for a bit more. I actually regret bringing you in.'

'No, you don't,' said Clarissa. 'This was tough. And I don't want to do it again. But we got Isabelle Isbister back. Gavin Isbister is no longer wronged. They don't do that to one of our own.'

'No, they don't,' said Macleod.

He took the cup off Clarissa after she'd drained it, and carrying the bag, started to walk back towards the car. Clarissa fell into step beside him in a way that only former police constables on the beat could ever do.

'There is one thing,' said Clarissa. 'I had to lose my hair for this and it's going to take a while to come back. I want to know what you're going to be doing to make up. What are you going to do about my lack of hair?'

'It's easy,' said Macleod as he walked off. 'I've collected all the hair I've lost from your driving. You can have it any time.'

He felt the punch, and then heard her wince, pain across her shoulders, but he turned and saw her smile. That was good.

He hadn't lost her through all of this. Clarissa was still Clarissa. He hoped they would all stay that way.

Read on to discover the Patrick Smythe series!

THE WOMAN ON THE MARINA

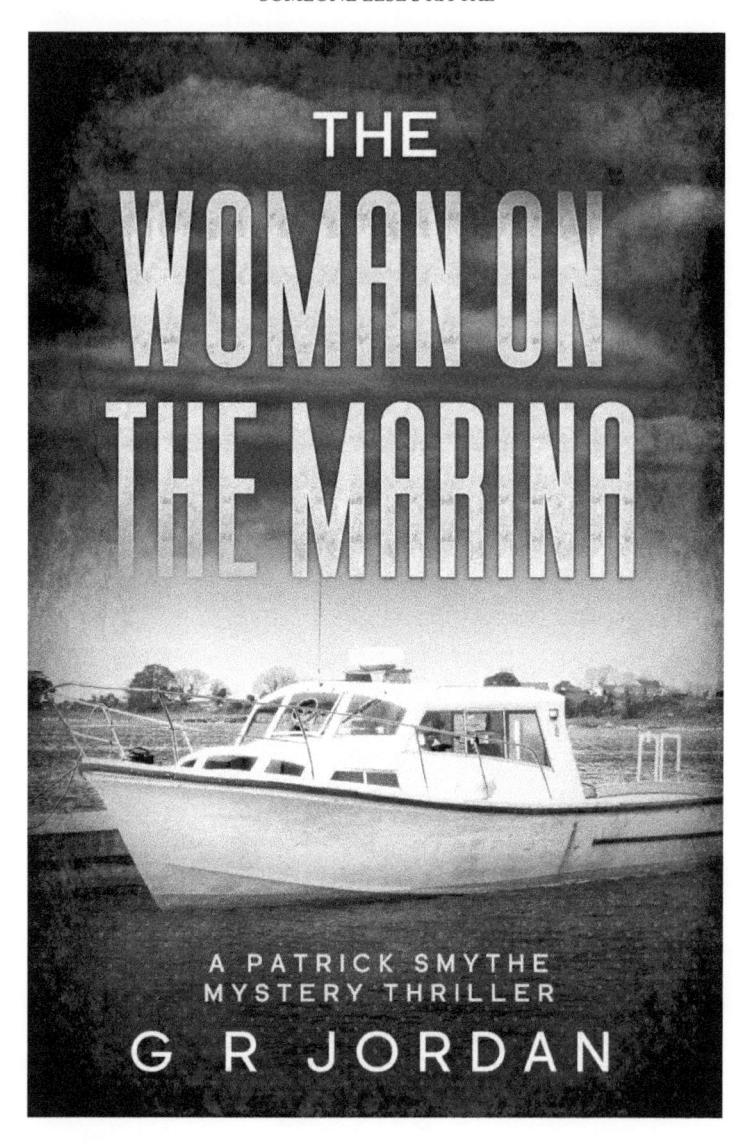

A PATRICK SMYTHE MYSTERY THRILLER

G R JORDAN

Patrick Smythe is a former Northern Irish policeman who after suffering an amputation after a bomb blast, takes to the sea between the west coast of Scotland and his homeland to ply his trade as a private investigator. Join Paddy as he tries to work to his own ethics while knowing how to bend the rules he once enforced. Working from his beloved motorboat 'Craigantlet', Paddy decides to rescue a drug mule in this short story from the pen of G R Jordan.

Join G R Jordan's monthly newsletter about forthcoming releases and special writings for his tribe of avid readers and then receive your free Patrick Smythe short story.

Go to https://bit.ly/PatrickSmythe for your Patrick Smythe journey to start!

About the Author

GR Jordan is a self-published author who finally decided at forty that in order to have an enjoyable lifestyle, his creative beast within would have to be unleashed. His books mirror that conflict in life where acts of decency contend with self-promotion, goodness stares in horror at evil, and kindness blindsides us when we at our worst. Corrupting our world with his parade of wondrous and horrific characters, he highlights everyday tensions with fresh eyes whilst taking his methodical, intelligent mainstays on a roller-coaster ride of dilemmas, all the while suffering the banter of their provocative sidekicks.

A graduate of Loughborough University where he masqueraded as a chemical engineer but ultimately played American football, Gary had worked at changing the shape of cereal flakes and pulled a pallet truck for a living. Watching vegetables freeze at -40'C was another career highlight and he was also one of the Scottish Highlands "blind" air traffic controllers.

These days he has graduated to answering a telephone to people in trouble before telephoning other people to sort it out.

Having flirted with most places in the UK, he is now based in the Isle of Lewis in Scotland where his free time is spent between raising a young family with his wife, writing, figuring out how to work a loom and caring for a small flock of chickens. Luckily, his writing is influenced by his varied work and life experience as the chickens have not been the poetical inspiration he had hoped for!

You can connect with me on:
🌐 https://grjordan.com
📘 https://facebook.com/carpetlessleprechaun

Subscribe to my newsletter:
✉ https://bit.ly/PatrickSmythe

Also by G R Jordan

G R Jordan writes across multiple genres including crime, dark and action adventure fantasy, feel good fantasy, mystery thriller and horror fantasy. Below is a selection of his work. Whilst all books are available across online stores, signed copies are available at his personal shop.

None Too Precious (Highlands & Islands Detective Book 44)
https://grjordan.com/product/none-too-precious
Babies snatched from their prams. Adult bodies left by the roadside. Can DI Hope McGrath find the connection and bring the children safely home?

When a body left on the A9 is found to be the uncle of a kidnapped child, Hope McGrath smells a connection between two terrifying crimes. As the pattern repeats and the children are not released, a terrifying public ultimatum is issued from a familiar foe. Can Hope and her team find the vengeful killer before the children suffer the same end as their relatives?

If you turn your back, they just keep raising the stakes!

Kirsten Stewart Thrillers
https://grjordan.com/product/a-shot-at-democracy

Join Kirsten Stewart on a shadowy ride through the underbelly of the Highlands of Scotland where among the beauty and splendour of the majestic landscape lies corruption and intrigue to match any city. From murders to extortion, missing children to criminals operating above the law, the Highland former detective must learn a tougher edge to her work as she puts her own life on the line to protect those who cannot defend themselves.

Having left her beloved murder investigation team far behind, Kirsten has to battle personal tragedy and loss while adapting to a whole new way of executing her duties where your mistakes are your own. As Kirsten comes to terms with working with the new team, she often operates as the groups solo field agent, placing herself in danger and trouble to rescue those caught on the dark side of life. With action packed scenes and tense scenarios of murder and greed, the Kirsten Stewart thrillers will have you turning page after page to see your favourite Scottish lass home!

There's life after Macleod, but a whole new world of death!

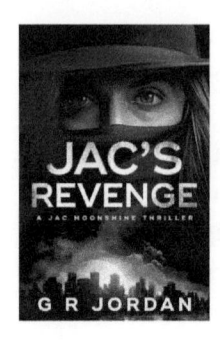

Jac's Revenge (A Jac Moonshine Thriller #1)

https://grjordan.com/product/jacs-revenge

An unexpected hit makes Debbie a widow. The attention of her man's killer spawns a brutal yet classy alter ego. But how far can you play the game before it takes over your life?

All her life, Debbie Parlor lived in her man's shadow, knowing his work was never truly honest. She turned her head from news stories and rumours. But when he was disposed of for his smile to placate a rival crime lord, Jac Moonshine was born. And when Debbie is paid compensation for her loss like her car was written off, Jac decides that enough is enough.

Get on board with this tongue-in-cheek revenge thriller that will make you question how far you would go to avenge a loved one, and how much you would enjoy it!

A Giant Killing (Siobhan Duffy Mysteries #1)
https://grjordan.com/product/a-giant-killing
A body lies on the Giant's boot. Discord, as the master of secrets has been found. Can former spy Siobhan Duffy find the killer before they execute her former colleagues?

When retired operative Siobhan Duffy sees the killing of her former master in the paper, her unease sends her down a path of discovery and fear. Aided by her young housekeeper and scruff of a gardener, Siobhan begins a quest to discover the reason for her spy boss' death and unravels a can of worms today's masters would rather keep closed. But in a world of secrets, the difference between revenge and simple, if brutal, housekeeping becomes the hardest truth to know.

The past is a child who never leaves home!

www.ingramcontent.com/pod-product-compliance
Ingram Content Group UK Ltd.
Pitfield, Milton Keynes, MK11 3LW, UK
UKHW041836220425
5574UKWH00001B/35